"A disturbir
time-shiftinç
ism and hun
thor of _Bar_

"Deeply affecting and profound, this accomplished novella oozes mystery and menace as it delves into the horrors of the past - and of the present. " **Essie Fox, author of _Dangerous_ and _The Fascination_**

"Cli-fi meets _Wuthering Heights_. Like the peat of the moorlands, this novella is darkly beautiful, multi-layered, and disturbed. It will get under your fingernails." **Clare Pollard, author of _The Modern Fairies_**

"Frightening and vivid - a siren song to humanity set against a much-loved and endangered landscape. I'll be thinking about this for a long time. " **Stacey Halls, author of _The Household_ and _Mrs England_**

"A powerful, beautifully written tale told with exquisite tenderness. The haunting story of a woman lost to herself who, as darkness closes in, unearths the truth of her life. " **Suzannah Dunn, author of _Levitation for Beginners_**

Turbine 34

Katherine Clements

Wild Hunt Books

Turbine 34
First published in 2025 by Wild Hunt Books
wildhuntbooks.co.uk

A CIP catalogue record for this title is available from the British Library

Paperback: 978-1-0685631-4-0
Ebook: 978-1-0685631-5-7

Cover Design by Luísa Dias
Edited by Ariell Cacciola
Typeset by Wild Hunt Books

The Northern Weird Project is a registered trademark of Wild Hunt Books

For my Dad, who loves these moors.

Day 1

Easting: 398146 Northing: 433524

Fuck, it's so hot.

She wriggles the backpack's straps away from the sore patches on her shoulders, shifts its weight hip to hip, sweat pooling in the hollow of her back. Up ahead, the turbine stretches skyward, a skeletal giant, limbs rotating lazily.

She should've known the pack was too heavy for this distance, this heat – should've hitched a ride with one of the estate staff – but she'd wanted to arrive at the site on foot. Alone. Approaching by the access track in the climate-controlled bubble of a slick new 4x4 had seemed wrong. She'd wanted to take the old route. The one scored into her bones, imprinted in her blood. She'd wanted to feel the moortop wind in her hair, to tread familiar paths, feel familiar earth beneath her boots, like a hefted sheep. And she's nothing if not determined.

Her father's Yorkshire burr conjures from deep memory: *You're bloody-minded as a cull yow, Lass.*

It's not as if she can get lost here. She recognises the horizon's silhouette, the ridgeline of each distant fell, the deep, shadowy cut of the valleys, the murmur of traffic from the road over the tops. She'd forgotten though, how hard going this terrain can be. How easily the tussocked moor grass turns ankles, how footholds that appear solid are anything but, how the only sure footing is the stepping stone roots of desiccated heather, which should be flowering now, but is mostly parched and stunted, a few lavender blooms struggling from baked peat.

She feels the dull stirrings of a migraine behind her right eye. Her meds are stashed at the bottom of the pack. A stupid oversight. There's no way to reach them without excavating carefully organised strata of clean underwear and dried food, Petri dishes and field equipment. Then re-packing it all and hoisting the damn thing back onto her shoulders. She pulls her t-shirt away from her sweat-slicked chest, gropes for the water bottle that's been banging arrhythmically against a loose carabiner on the pack and takes a long draw.

God, that's better.

She checks the GPS again. Yes, that's the one: Turbine 34.

She'd know anyway, without navigation. She'd know this place by the contour of the land. The scent. Even with the heat and drought, she can still detect the rich peaty soil deep beneath her feet, the savour of rusty becks and silica-glittering gritstone, the cotton grass and animal scat. Something's missing though – the full-body gunshot shock of grouse bursting from cover, like catapulted umbrellas. There aren't many left these days. Just some stubborn old timers who've outlived the guns.

Away to her left, the access track is a great scar across the moor – a broad scrape of rubble and sand, as if God has gouged it with a fingernail. She's seen drone footage, of course, the winding tracks leading to each turbine forming a bird's-eye Kandinsky. What the film couldn't reveal was the smaller debris, the left-behind detritus of construction: chips of aggregate and hardcore; fragments of plastic and steel; the great humps of displaced, upturned peat, rock and sand hunkered by each turbine, gradually reclaimed by moss and lichen, remoulding the landscape like ancient burial mounds. Nor the changes beneath ground – the dried-up dykes and grips, the deep fissures and clefts in the peat's surface, and the massive steel and concrete foundations squatting beneath the bog like backfilled bunkers.

No – up close, the moor is not how she remembers it. Something essential has changed.

As a child she'd filled countless scrapbooks with sky-lark sightings, mapped the tracks of fox and deer, collected and pressed wildflowers. She'd waited patiently each spring for the curlews' return – their first tremulous calls making her heart burst. And through the long hours, she'd never, ever felt alone.

Now, it's eerily quiet. No walkers. No birdsong. No small, panicked creatures scurrying away from her clumsy tread. Between the tussocks, the peat is as desiccated as an overbaked cake. Her boots stay dry. Mind you, that's not surprising, the summer they've had.

Hottest on record, they're predicting. Hotter even than 2032, the current drought lasting over three months. Reservoirs are dry, crops have failed, water companies enforcing cuts, the first deaths by heatstroke and dehydration.

She'd followed the clickbait, tapping a screen over lunch at the off-campus Pret, far enough from the labs to avoid curious student eyes. Warnings about Atlantic hurricanes and brewing storms with portentous biblical names like Malachi and Ariel. The impending threat of devastating floods and wind damage. Communities destroyed. Lives lost. It's the same every year now. The cycle of drought and deluge. The heat will break, and the rain will come.

But it has to be now. This dry spell means she can camp out. She needs to be here through the dark hours, observing, listening, searching, when she knows no one else will be. That's what she wants more than anything – to be left alone to carry out the task she's been given. The task she's given herself.

It's been three years since they switched on the final turbine, seven since construction began.

There'd been significant progress on sustainable energy for a decade or more, but when the government had pushed hard for net zero and removed the constraints, the overseas conglomerates had seized their moment. They'd sent surveyors and slick salesmen with Saville Row suits and London accents to persuade every struggling farmer that wind and solar would save them. Let the cattle graze beneath windmills. Turn over arable land to panels. Imports are cheaper anyway, and the supermarkets care most about price.

But this – this project had been different. This one had made headlines.

She'd made environmental impact assessments of green energy projects her speciality, has been in the game since long before such things entered public discourse, knows intimately how the smallest shift in land use creates a cascade, sometimes predictable, sometimes not. She prides herself on her sensitive, well-bal-

anced conclusions, her clear-eyed approach, her ability
to avoid taking sides. It was inevitable she'd come here.
She'd known as she watched the local campaigners glue
themselves to the first towers and slip past security to
spoil fresh concrete foundations, the old hippies lying
down in front of the diggers. They knew, like she did,
that there was more at stake here than the spoiling of a
beloved landscape. This was not about aesthetics. Disturbing the protected peatland would have unforeseen
consequences that couldn't be planned for, couldn't be
mitigated. And that those losses could never be mend-
ed. She also knew that their fight was futile, that there
were larger forces at play, and that no one could stop
what had begun hundreds of years before in these valleys.

She'd followed the court cases, read about the
heavy-handed security and protestors' prison sentences,
the lives ruined. And she'd waited, patiently, knowing
the job would be hers, knowing they'd need someone
before they knew it themselves. An expert to measure
and record and evaluate. Someone dispassionate and
disconnected from the rumour and scandal. Someone
neutral to determine whether the valley's devastating
floods were a direct result of the wind farm's construction, or would they have happened anyway?

She can already guess the answer. Can read it in the
grim local faces she saw as she walked through town,

past boarded-up shops and shuttered pubs, a few disappointed tourists eating pasties in the square, the abandoned terraces near the river, now mouldering, the old civic buildings ring-marked with tidelines, riddled with black mould and hazard signs, and the medieval packhorse bridge that had crumbled into the river after 500 years of service. No funds to restore it.

She'd trekked up to the rain-battered graveyard to find family headstones – aunts, uncles, cousins. Fading half-remembered names. But not her own parents. They'd sold up and moved away, of course, not long after she'd gone. Buried now, under gentler, chalky soil.

She finds the one she wants beside an ostentatious headstone in black marble. Next door, Cousin Jim rests beneath local stone. Name. Dates. No fuss. He'd have wanted it that way. Nearby, fake yellow roses and bright plastic pens litter the grave of the famous dead poet. There used to be a real rose here, she recalls. A surprising joyful burst of colour on the grey mizzled hilltop. Gone now, like the rest of them.

She clicks the water bottle back into place, steadies herself. It's the noise that's the worst thing. The electrical hum, like a motorway or a high-flying jet. A mechanical, human noise, at odds with the landscape. Cloud shadows chase across distant hills, streaks of ochre and auburn, veridian green and russet brown, a lone glowing patch of violet catching the sun. The pale bones of other turbines like this one. She listens for the telltale burble of running water, but the dykes are dry, the old drainage ditches stagnant. She'll have to walk to find a fresh spring.

She sets off again, picking her way across uneven ground. Fifty metres from the turbine platform she misjudges a step and her ankle twists beneath her. Time expands. She knows she's going to fall before it happens, attempts to pitch toward a springy patch of heather, unbalanced by the weight on her back, and topples with a thud, breath knocked out of her.

Fuck. Not a good start.

She checks herself. No livid pain. No cracking sounds. She steadies her breath, lets her body readjust. Lies there sucking the air back into her lungs. This close to the earth, the damp, dense scent of the ancient peat reaches her. As regular as a heartbeat, the shadow of the turbine's rotating blades falls across her. A momentary dimming of sunlight. A lamp switching off and on.

She's fine, she decides. Bruised, undoubtably – she bruises so easily these days – but no lasting damage. She unclips the buckles at chest and hip, slides her shoulders from the pack's tethers and levers herself onto her knees, then, slowly, to her feet. Her ankle complains.

A sharp stab behind her left kneecap – old news. She hoists the pack upright. Detects no telltale tinkle of shattered glass or cracked plastic. *Thank God.* She cares more about the fragile equipment than she does her old bones.

Not far to go, but she daren't drag it – not after that jolt. So, she lifts, legs quivering, and shoulders the damn thing once more.

The turbine platform is a flat stretch of rough, rubbled ground. At one end, the access track marks the way out. How much aggregate, steel and hardcore had it taken to create this incongruous plateau? She knows the answer, of course, but can't bring the numbers to mind. The fall has made her thick-headed, or maybe she's dehydrated. Her skull thumps dully.

At least the flat ground is a reliable place to set up base camp. She chooses a spot at the far edge from the turbine and lowers the pack, the relief making her weightless. She should've known better than to bring the old red tent with its heavy frame and weighty groundsheet, but she'd felt impulsive; surely she can allow herself some nostalgia. More water first, but not too much, not until she's located the nearest source.

Now she's close, the noise takes on a different timbre, a complexity of sounds: the bass rumble of a generator, the grinding of gears, the occasional mechanical squeal, like the echo of a distant factory. The turning blades make a rhythmic whoosh, like passing cars, or waves against a pebbled beach.

She walks over and stands beneath the turbine's blades. From inside the huge tower comes a flurry of clicks. Above, the nacelle with its nubbed nose and the dizzying sight of the blades, already dirtied by weather and pollution, pale grey against the blue, blue sky. She's reminded of a white cedar tree she once saw in the ghost forests of New Jersey – a huge, once-impressive thing, now leafless and haunting, a phantom of its former self, destroyed by the salt incursion of rising sea levels.

She circles the turbine. The transformer – a garden hut sized box of riveted metal – sits close by. Scrawled across one wall, the pink ghost of painted over graffiti:

PLANET NOT PROFIT

OFFSHORE NOT ONSHORE

FUCK OFF WUTHERING SHITES!

And of course, the obligatory cock and balls.

She's stood, like this, beneath countless turbines, but she's never prepared for the disorientation, the way it seems that the blades will somehow reach down and slice through her. The shudder of discomfort and compulsion to move away. The eerie, lonely music they make. She turns and leans back against the turbine's steel tower, feels a juddering vibration from within. The metal is hot in the sun, stark and industrial. She shuts her eyes, concentrates on the sun's heat on her cheeks. Up here, at least there's a breeze, as if the humid air is stirred by the turbine's turning. She can smell something acrid – grease, perhaps, or oil – and the tang of hot metal, but beneath that, a scent more pungent and pervading. She recognises it and smiles to herself. An ancient, familiar perfume that even this extent of human interference can't erase. Dark and earthy, damp and musky. Reminiscent of badger sets and fox dens, of moss and mire and mushroom, of cold starlit nights and smouldering peat fires. Of old things, long-buried and long-forgotten.

Night

A scream wakes her. A violent, desperate cry – the sound of someone fighting for their life. She claws her way out of the sleeping bag, heart clattering, gulping for breath, fugged in the familiar hot-cold delirium of night sweats. The darkness is absolute, a black velvet blindfold. She fumbles for the lantern that she'd left by her head, clicks it on, and the tent floods with a reassuring womb-like glow.

She does what Doctor Kagehira taught her. Start with the breath. Deep and slow. One at a time. Count the inhale: one-two. Extend the out: one-two-three-four.

I am safe. I am safe. I am safe.

Of course the dream would return now, sleeping in such unfamiliar circumstances. Any change of routine can trigger it. But still, it's been at least three years since the last episode, and she'd thought she was done. Night terrors, that's what Doctor Kagehira had called them. Always the same: strangulating pressure on her windpipe, suffocating dank soil filling her mouth, heart-pounding panic, her body convulsing as she *can't breathe–can't breathe–can't breathe*.

She checks her watch. 1.07am. A few hours till dawn.

She listens to the hum of the turbine transformer, the movement of the blades, until her heartbeat slows and synchronises with their rhythmic swoosh. Inhale: one-two. Exhale: one-two-three-four.

I am safe. I am safe. I am safe.

Calmer, she wriggles back down into her sleeping bag, ignoring the sickly fevered sensation that accompanies the tail end of the dream. The lantern can stay on.

She's starting to drift when a sound brings her back. A scream, distinctly and unmistakably human. A woman.

She's bolt upright, heart wild. *That was real.*

She holds her breath, concentrates on each steady swoop of the turbine's blades. And sure enough, it comes again – a wild and urgent high-pitched cry.

Icy needles sweep from the pit of her stomach and stab at her heart.

What the fuck is that?

Above the turbine's hum she picks out the feint breath of moortop breeze, the lonely hoot of an owl in the valley below.

She knows better than this. Knows that everything can be explained. Understands the basic physics of sound waves, the anatomy of the ear, the neuroscience of dreaming. The recurring dream always sends her spiralling, makes her unsure of her senses. It takes a while for her body to settle. She knows this.

Another loud, desperate shriek pierces the night, closer this time. Too close.

Fuck this.

She forces herself out of the sleeping bag and crawls to the tent's entrance, grabs the torch she'd left there, hesitates only a second before unzipping the inner, then the fly – the metal zip seeming shatteringly loud – and directs the bright LED beam into the darkness.

All she can see is the flat expanse of the access platform, littered with chunks of grey rock like the surface of the moon, the pale cylinder of Turbine 34 at the far end, ghostly in the beam's furthest reach.

Another shrill cry sounds behind her, some distance to the north. Her body wills her to crawl back inside the tent, hide inside the sleeping bag, pretend this isn't happening. There must be a rational explanation. Foxes, perhaps. Or some other animal drama playing out in the nightly dance of life and death. But it doesn't sound like foxes, doesn't have the right pitch. Lacks the cry-baby scream of fighting cats. It sounds all too human.

But if there is someone out here, she needs to know. She won't be frightened off on the first night.

She climbs out of the tent, wincing at a tweak of pain from her twisted ankle, stands barefoot in nothing but cotton shorts and a sweat-damp vest, and turns 360, skimming the torch beam over the landscape. The moor expands and contracts around her, the rich greens and golds and browns desaturated by the artificial light, making everything filtered and unreal.

The scream comes again, this time off to the east and she spins toward it, expecting to spotlight the phosphorescent luminosity of hungry animal eyes.

Christ, what is it? Who *is it?*

Maybe it *is* foxes, but she's never known them call to each other that way. Could it be birds? She's never heard a bird make that sound. Some other creature killing rabbits? What could be hunting so broadly? Moving so swiftly?

The torch beam hits a white shape and her heart judders. There's something over there, to the east, looming through the darkness, something pale and...

She follows the turbine tower skyward, glimpses the white blades rotating slowly. She hears it again. A scream. No, not a scream this time. The sharp discordant squeal of metal on metal.

Her body floods with relief.

She drops to her knees, trembling, laughing, almost tearful.

What on earth was she thinking? How could she be so stupid? The dream has dissembled her perceptions, scrambled her senses. It's not like her to let her imagination run wild like this. When she was younger, sure, but over the years she's learned to suppress her superstitious, pagan side, to quiet the frightened little girl who once believed in stories of ghosts and boggarts and moor-sprites. She prides herself on rationality, her sensible, scientific brain. She was well-trained, after all – it was one of the first things he'd taught her.

The first time he'd noticed her was the autumn term, second year of sixth form college.

He was the kind of teacher who raised eyebrows among the parents. Old enough to remember the Clangers the first-time round, young enough to use Clearasil. Black, ill-fitting jumble sale blazers, by choice rather than necessity. An unruly mass of curls died Nice & Easy Midnight. His looks evoked the gangs of goths who loitered in the park – more rock star than science nerd. She'd once overheard someone say so at an open evening. 'Rock star?' Came the incredulous reply. 'Undertaker, more like.'

Old people. What did they know?

He reminded her of those mysterious musicians who glowered from the pages of NME, eyelinered and backcombed, a whiff of Bryon and Shelley and Keats. It was the intense stare, the second-hand cravats and the propensity for peppering A-level biology lessons with literature references that had captivated her. He was the cool one. Call me Kent. No Mister.

'What kinda name is that?' her best mate Sally had scoffed, after their first lesson with him. 'And that accent. Jeez.'

She'd thought it romantic, his southern vowels and clipped pronunciation evoking posh schools where boys wore bow ties, and big country houses of butter-yellow stone with stable blocks where grooms had once tumbled with ladies' maids. She'd said as much.

'Christ – where'd you get this shit?'

He was so much more sophisticated than the local lads, who huffed superglue from paper bags and tried to get high smoking dried banana skins. He was The Jesus and Mary Chain, The Velvet Underground and Jeff Buckley. He was absinthe in a dark bar and Withnail and Doc Martens. He was twenty John Player Special. He was Robert Smith's kohl. He was Sylvia Plath's grave. He was – she decided – *a poet*.

Sally had cackled at this.

'But science *is* poetry. Why can't I like both?'

That conviction has never left her. Now, she finds rhythm and metre in the minutiae of a spoil sample, rhyme in the Latin nomenclature scattered throughout her days, beauty and meaning in the changes wrought by forces so much larger than herself, awe in human powerlessness, hope in the persistence of life.

He had understood all that. Had conceived such thoughts in her and cultivated them.

The first time he had touched her was in lab, the third week of term. Petrie dishes of soil samples under microscopes. She and Sally – of course, it was always Sally – had collected their samples from beneath the small stand of birch trees at the edge of the car park, distancing themselves from the others who had all headed to the turfed and pesticide-sprayed monoculture of the playing fields. She was crooked, eye to the viewer, immersed in the new world she had discovered, when she smelt him – cigarettes, charity-shop clothes, patchouli and something else – something unfamiliar, feral and musky that made her crotch tingle.

'Can I see?' he'd asked, cocking a brow. A half-smile that made his cheek dimple. *Lord, what a smile.*

She nodded, hung back as he put one eye to the viewfinder, pale knuckles gripping the wooden bench either side. *Hands of an artist.* Long lean fingers, nails bitten to the stub, unscarred and uncalloused, the opposite of the male hands she was used to, belonging to farm labourers and mechanics, blackened with engine grease and cow shit – the men of her family.

'You chose well,' he said, lifting his head and appraising her. 'Plenty to explore here. Lots of bacteria. Some protozoa. Well done. See how many you can identify.'

He smiled again, and stepped back, allowing her to return to the microscope, the air between them all sparks. As she bent to the viewer, tucking a wayward hank of dark hair behind her ear, his fingers momentarily brushed the small slice of exposed skin at the curve of her back, between her jeans and t-shirt. An accident perhaps, to anyone watching, but she knew it wasn't. She knew right away what it meant.

Day 2

The probe meets resistance. There's something hard buried in the peat. Carefully, she extracts the metal cylinder. Through the plastic window she studies the peat core, measures back the decades: the colour of tea leaves where the sun has scorched the last 100 years, a rich, oily black in centuries past. At the tip, somewhere in the mid-seventeenth century – pre-industrial, certainly – she spies flecks of a pale substance mingled with the soil. Slowly, she presses the plunger to release the first inch or two into a sample dish. She's right – there are tiny specks of hard, yellowish grit between her fingers. It could be anything really – an old deposit of quarried stone, crumbling animal bone – but there's certainly something down there. Something that isn't peat. This is a good place to start.

She sets down a quadrat and marks out a square, takes the small trowel from her backpack and sets to work, gently excavating around the dead roots of a bilberry, selecting samples at random.

It's hot work, the sun blazing, the upper layers of peat dry and compacted. There's no sign of the heatwave abating, barely a cloud in the sky. Nearby, Turbine 34 rotates lazily. At least up here there's a breeze, enough to make the thing spin. It's surprising she's seen no one all day – no ramblers, no dog walkers, no runners. It's probably too hot for most. Down in the valley tourists will be sweltering over melted Mr Whippy and complaining about the lack of air conditioning. Even at this elevation, the heat makes her sweat, the sun crisping the back of her neck. Regardless, she works slowly, carefully removing the vegetation, the star moss and sundew clinging on in the cotton grass, exposing the youngest peat. It crumbles between her fingers, dry and dusty as stale breadcrumbs, but she finds the remains of a snail shell, miniscule tendrils of fungi, a clutch of pearlescent slug eggs, glistening like buried treasure. Proof of life. Reassuring.

She'd expected to find a significant impact on soil quality, moisture content and carbon storage capacity, she'd expected to find things altered; what she hadn't been prepared for was the subtle but disconcerting sense of absence – a space where life should be. The moor in summer was always a noisy place, eloquent with the constant commotion of bird song. If it wasn't the grouse, then it was the skylarks, the redshank and snipe, the golden plover, the lapwings and curlews. The constant busyness of fledging and feathers.

That morning, as she'd sat at the tent's entrance, bandaging her swollen ankle, slapping away midges and cursing gently under her breath, she'd realised what was missing. Whatever birdcall might reach her is mostly drowned out by the turbine's incessant whoosh, the generator's hum and the ear-close buzz of proliferating insects. Without the birds, the place seems strangely desolate – a true wasteland.

She's patient, methodological, as always. Absorbed in her work. The stack of plastic dishes grows by her side. Later, she'll take them back to the lab, and study them under a microscope, entering a world that feels like home. If the peat is healthy, it will be teeming with life, with bacteria and fungi, viruses and archaea, microscopic life forms that can't be seen with the naked eye but are responsible for the formation of the peat itself. It's these miniscule miracle workers who break down the sphagnum to create the bog. She'll send samples for metagenomic analysis, looking for evidence of shifts in the delicate make-up of the soil microbiome. Feed the fresh data to specialist AI models, so her findings can be transformed into predictions and certainties. She's grateful she gets to see the world this way – up close – is always amazed by the extent of critical life in one tiny sample of soil. How, without these invisible organisms in their sightless underworld, all of animal life would cease to exist. The breathless beauty of it. The synchronicity. The heart-pounding horror at life's fragility. Biology as poetry.

When she stops to take a drink, she notices another huge turbine, several hundred metres away, standing motionless. It's the one that had woken her in the night. Its blades are still and splayed, as if pleading with the gods of wind for attention. If she focuses, she can just pick out the whir of a generator, the mechanism straining as it attempts to gain traction. In the daylight it sounds like squealing brakes. How could she have thought otherwise?

She's excavated two feet down before the trowel hits something hard. She finds a pale, yellowish stain in the fragile earth, and gently scrapes around it with the patience of an archaeologist, determined not to contaminate whatever it is.

Slowly she uncovers a long straight patch of pale material, culminating in a larger, circular bulb that reminds her of a parietal bone – the rear of a human skull. Her heart patters as a fragment chips away beneath the pressure of her trowel. *Damn. Be careful.* She grabs her magnifier. As she focuses her heart sinks. The texture is porous and lumpy, crumbling easily.

Fucking concrete. Are you kidding me?

Frustrated she scrapes harder, exposing a larger chunk that she levers from its resting place.

Yep – definitely concrete. For fucks sake.

She lobs the thing in the heather. The whole site is littered with the stuff. The dregs and leftovers of construction. Accidental spills, excesses, bad mixes – the contractors had probably just churned it all back into the ground. She'd thought this spot had lain undisturbed for decades, even centuries, practically virgin blanket bog, but clearly not. And that means her samples are useless. She's misjudged it. She should've been more selective. And she should've expected this. After all, she'd collected great chunks of aggregate and hardcore from the access platform while clearing a space for her tent, enough to make a midden at one end of the clearing. She could build a cairn to commemorate her mistakes.

As she makes her way back to the tent, she hears barking.

There are two dogs: the larger, a white and tan pointer; the smaller, a shaggy little terrier of some sort.

The pointer is chasing the terrier, driving it into frenzied yapping. In the distance, three figures stride the moor. One of them shouts for the dogs but is ignored, and the animals come pelting toward her.

They're the first people she's seen since she arrived, and she suddenly feels a possessive indignation. She's already proprietorial about this stretch of moorland and is irritated by their trespass.

By the time she reaches the firm footing of the turbine platform, she can see the intruders better. Two men and a young boy. The men are both dressed in the earthy browns and greens of woollen tweed, flat caps and leather boots, even in this heat. She'd expected to see splashes of the brightly coloured Gore-Tex favoured by seasoned walkers, the reflective vests of fell runners, or the branded t-shirts and impractical sandals of ill-equipped tourists trying to find their way to some place or another. These men in their traditional country gear seem an anomaly. Especially now, in the dying days of an August heat wave. As they come closer she realises that both men have shotguns broken over their elbows.

It's been years since this place hosted shoots – birds and turbines don't mix – but they must be gamekeepers. Must be, though she knows the estate staff no longer carry weapons. There's no need. The birds are mostly gone, and with them, the predators. Besides, the keepers she's used to dealing with come in two flavours: Barbour or North Face. Land Rover or quad bike. These two look like caricatures from some bygone age, extras from *Downton Abbey*.

The staff have been instructed to leave her alone. To give her a wide berth, as she'd requested. She doesn't want them tramping all over the site or churning up the peat in their four-wheel drives. The dogs are another matter. They race toward her, bounding over the heather, the bigger chasing the smaller. The boy comes running after them. A flurry of finches rises in a panicked burst of feathers, chattering into the sky, deftly skirting the turbine's blades. A happy surprise.

As the terrier nears her, she bends, expecting the barrelling breathless excitement she associates with small dogs, but it pulls up short about ten metres away and starts to bark. It weaves side to side, ears flattened, its high yapping echoing across the moor. The pointer draws up behind it, sharp eyes fixed in her direction, sniffing the air.

It's only natural they should be mistrustful – probably working dogs, suspicious of strangers. A wave of disappointment surges through her. She still misses the dogs of her childhood. The simplicity of her relationship with them.

She stoops, hands on knees, making herself smaller and less threatening 'Hi there. Do you want to be friends?' One hand, outstretched in mimic of a treat. No success. Instead, the terrier stiffens and growls.

The men have stopped. One of them shades his eyes and squints in her direction. She straightens and raises a hand, but he doesn't acknowledge her.

He calls the dogs to heel, and the pointer responds, looks back toward its master, back to her, then wheels away. The terrier stays, teeth bared, trembling with aggression.

She bends again, holds out a conciliatory hand. 'It's OK. I won't hurt you.'

The boy comes puffing up behind the dog. 'Frank, do come on...'

He's a peculiar looking child – perhaps nine or ten, freckled with a head of wind-whipped ginger curls. He's wearing short trousers, socks pulled up to his knees, and a knitted vest that could only be described as a pullover.

'Hello there!' she says with a smile.

The boy ignores her. Instead, he addresses the dog. 'Whatever's the matter, Frank? What's wrong with you?'

Frank remains fixated on her.

'He doesn't seem to like me,' she says, trying to keep her tone light and friendly. She's always been awkward with children.

Again, the boy ignores her. He's probably been taught to avoid strangers, too.

Instead, he tuts and tries to grab the dog by its collar. It darts away and quivers, snarling at her.

One of the men sounds a whistle – a sudden piercing shriek that makes her flinch. This does the trick. The dog hesitates, all trembling fur and teeth, then yelps and makes off across the moor. The boy sighs, turns and follows it, shoulders slumped.

'Bye, then!' she calls. No acknowledgement.

Probably his way of telling her she's not welcome here. She ignores a niggling sense of unease. She's used to interactions like this. Men who claim to care about the land they steward but who don't believe in prying scientists, have no time for talk of climate change and global warming, who raise eyebrows at words like bio-diversity and ecosystem, their hostility evident in terse conversation and defensive body language. Once, she'd been threatened at gun point by a keeper on a Scottish estate – a gnarled old man who spoke a peculiar blend of English and Gaelic and looked as if he'd never left the hillside he found her on. It took a long and wearing walk back to the truck to show him the equipment before he'd believe that they'd let a woman up there to work all alone. He'd kept his ancient gun to her back all the way, as if he were walking some escaped convict back to jail.

Not surprising then that those men would act that way. She doesn't care. She shrugs it off these days. She no longer needs to be liked.

It's only later, as darkness falls and she watches the lights blink on in the valley, that she realises: humans can't hear dog whistles.

Night

She can't sleep. She lies there, hoping to hear curlew song above the sound of Turbine 34. Even if she doesn't see one, she'd like to hear the hooping, vibrato call, to know that they are still here.

Her mind runs on. The oddness of her interaction with the dogs and their owners bothers her, has left behind an unsettling, dislocated feeling. Had she really heard the dog whistle, or had she imagined it? She thinks about the night before, the way her mind had conjured up horrors in the dark like some sort of neurotic jumping at shadows. It's not like her – at least, it's not how she used to be. Her head hurts again. Her sprained ankle throbs. As she turns, trying to get comfortable, she feels a shifting seasickness. Could the local campaigners be right – could these symptoms be the effect of infrasound?

She's read countless studies on the impacts of low-frequency noise – the dizziness, fatigue and anxiety reported by communities living in proximity to wind turbines – and taken them with a pinch of salt. The science linking turbines to a host of health complaints is still patchy, no funding for research that doesn't fit the narrative. Sensationalist stories of people suffering un-explained feelings of dread, depression, even paranoia, read like propaganda from those pushing an extreme agenda. Fake news. A few articles in the broadsheets accusing the green energy industry of cover-ups have, so far, failed to rouse any legal action. She'd dismissed it. Now that she's here, she's not so sure. How else to explain the disorientating, immaterial sensation that plagues her? Maybe it's just the heat.

Her thoughts turn to the past. Long-buried mem-ories reawaken, of a time before all this, before she had imagined that the landscape she loved could ever be changed. Her father, blue overalls smeared with engine grease, trying to fix the old Massey Ferguson. Her mother, porridge-faced and blousy, laughing as she chased hens back into the coop. And of course, Kent.

The first time they'd been alone was the day he'd asked her to stay behind after class. As the others had filed out, he'd flicked his white lab coat aside as if it were a velvet frock coat and perched on his desk. He reached for a pack of Golden Virginia and extracted Rizlas, offered them to her. She shook her head, and the corner of his mouth twitched.

'It's OK. I don't give a shit. You're old enough anyway. Easily.'

She was. But she was clumsy with rollies and didn't want to look a fool – a child – in front of him. She'd never got the hang of them, despite Colin the farmhand trying to teach her. He'd laughed at her efforts, then just rolled them for her.

'No, ta. I'm fine.'

He extracted a paper, a pinch of tobacco. 'So, I wanted to speak to you privately.'

In her stomach, something took flight. Butterflies was too pretty a word. Something darker and more dangerous, with sharp claws and a ravenous appetite. Crows. Jackdaws. Vampire bats.

He rolled the cigarette with those long, pale fingers, brought the paper to his lips. His tongue – wet, pink, fleshy.

'That paper you turned in last week. Did you have help with it?'

'Help?'

'Yeah, did someone help you? Or did you, maybe, copy it from somewhere?'

'No.'

One eyebrow twitched, almost imperceptibly. 'You're sure?'

'Course.'

'It's OK if you did. I'm not going to tell anyone but I do need you to be honest with me.'

The blood crept hotly to her cheeks, a boil of indignation and confusion. 'What are you saying?'

'Well ... I was impressed.'

'Oh...'

'*Very* impressed.'

'OK...'

'If it *was* all your own work, then we need to talk.'

Her stomach gurgled audibly – that happened when she was nervous. She attempted a casual lean against the desk. 'It *was* all my own work, *honestly*.'

It was. She'd slaved over it. Spent a whole Saturday in Leeds University library.

He took a long drag on the cigarette and exhaled, his appraising gaze never leaving hers. He pushed the tobacco pouch toward her. 'Are you sure you don't want one?'

She nodded. What the fuck was this?

'OK then, tell me this. What do you want to do after college?'

'Erm... I don't know. Uni maybe, if I can get in.'

'What do you care about?'

'Sorry?'

'What are your passions? What turns you on?'

She focused on the glowing tip of the fag, the kiss of his lips as he exhaled. There was a look in his eye she couldn't read.

'I guess I like the usual stuff...'

He rolled his eyes. 'OK, let me put it like this. What's your favourite subject?'

'This one. Biology.'

'Why?'

Because of you. 'Erm ... I don't know.'

'Yes, you do.'

'I guess ... I guess I'm interested in why things are the way they are – the world I mean. The natural world. And how what *we* do changes that. What we can control. What we can't. This conservation stuff. I'm really interested in that.'

'Good. Those are big questions. Important questions.'

He studied her through the cigarette smoke as her brain darted. They were Sartre and de Beauvoir at a café table in Paris. They were Mary and Percy Shelley at the Villa Diodati. They were Plath and Hughes in the smoky corner of a Yorkshire pub.

'Have you decided where you're applying?'

'No.'

'Because, I think, if you work at it, if you start now, you could get into Oxbridge.'

'Oxbridge?'

'Oxford or Cambridge.'

God, she was an idiot. She'd laughed it off. 'That's ridiculous.'

'It's not.' He'd leant forward and placed a hand on her forearm – those beautiful fingers touching the fabric of her cardigan, but he might as well have stroked her breast. The effect it had, electric. Every cell thrumming.

'It's not ridiculous. Why would you think that?'

'Well ... I mean ... that's for rich folks.'

'There are grants. Loans. If I can do it, you can.'

'You went to Oxenbridge?'

'Oxbridge.' He released her arm, sat back. 'Yeah. I was at Oxford. Balliol.'

The dreaming spires. A fantasy ever since she'd read *Brideshead Revisited*. An impossibility that he suddenly made possible.

'Wow ... that's so cool.'

He pulled the Petri dish he used as an ashtray toward him and stubbed out the cigarette.

'Listen. I see something in you. Something the others don't have. You're clever, but you know that already. I see passion. The kind when you really love a subject. The kind that will take you wherever you want to go. Away from here, if that's what you want.'

She felt embarrassed. Childish. But deep down, a spark of recognition, of hope, as he put into words all her secret dreams. She'd never felt understood by boys her own age. Even with Colin that time, when he'd slid himself inside her and bellowed like a heifer about to give birth. This was different – a different kind of connection, as if he could read her mind.

'I wouldn't even know where to start.'

'Luckily, I do.' He stood, peeled off the lab coat and swapped it for the blazer that always hung on the back of his desk chair. She got a whiff of his musky, male scent, notes of fresh sweat and spice. 'Look, I'm not supposed to have favourites, obviously, and I'm not supposed to give more time to one student than any other, but I can help you, if you want. It'll just have to be between us, OK?'

'OK...'

'We'll have to cover extra stuff – stuff I won't bother teaching this lot. He waved an orchestral palm toward the empty lab. 'Free periods, after hours. Can you do that?'

God, yes! She nodded. Her parents barely knew where she was most of the time anyway.

'Good. Think about it over the weekend. Think about whether you really want this. Because I won't waste my time if you're not up for it.'

Christ, those turbulent eyes. She stopped herself from thinking about storm clouds – how trite. It was something more animalistic. Feral. Greedy. That goddamn bat trying to escape from her chest.

'I already know,' she said, understanding. 'I already know what I want.'

A startling sound interrupts her thoughts – stretching long across the moor, brim-full with hunger and melancholy – the plaintive howl of a wolf.

What the fuck? Was that real?

Foggy with lack of sleep, she rolls onto her back, the thin summer sleeping bag tangled round her legs. The wind is up, and a new thin whistle sounds above her head – the air trapped between the tent's layers.

The howl comes again, and this time is answered by another. The calls of a wolf pack. Unmistakable.

She drags herself to sitting and listens, skin prickling into goosebumps despite the muggy heat in the tent. After the previous night, she doesn't trust her senses. She blinks hard, sinks her nails into her palm. She's certainly awake. Her ankle throbs, her knees ache and there's the sharp twinge of sciatica that always flares whenever she sleeps in a strange bed.

The sound rises in a chorus, mournful and wanting. Several animals calling to each other, the way wolves do when they're hunting. Whatever it is, she's not imagining it this time.

It can't be wolves, of course, but it sounds like them. She's heard that sound only once before. Alaska. Part of a group of field scientists studying the seabird colony at Cape Lisburne. But then, there had been the wooden walls of a cabin and a lover's arms between her and the wild arctic tundra.

Johannes. Quiet and serious. Surprisingly adventurous in bed. He'd held her tighter as they'd listened in wonder to the wolf chorus echoing across the ice. It had seemed a charmed moment, achingly wild, staggeringly beautiful. She'd been happy there, in that stark world of freezing waterfalls tinkling with icicles, delicate alpine blooms and the swirling hues of the aurora borealis – the kind of place wolves *should* be.

But they shouldn't – *couldn't* – be here. Her hackles rise.

She's familiar with fear in other contexts, of course, after a lifetime of ingrained caution at every unlit, empty street, every deserted car park, each sideways look and 'accidental' touch, but she's never been truly frightened in the wild. Men are the things to be most scared of. Not animals. Since she turned fifty, even the mundane urban fears have lessened. She's slowly becoming invisible, unseen by male predators. There is freedom in that. The kind of freedom that has allowed her to make audacious decisions and demands like this one – to work alone. Choices that, as a younger woman, she might not have made. Is she fearless? Not quite. Not yet. That would be stupid. Braver, certainly. But, sitting in the pitch black of the tent, senses hyper-alert, prickling with tension, that bravery is exposed as a lie.

Dogs. It must be. It can't be anything else. She thinks of the gamekeepers' dogs she'd seen earlier – the terrier and the pointer. There must be others too, scattered at nearby farms and converted barns. Something must have set them off, calling to each other.

Are there feral dogs out here? Is that possible? Family pets gone missing and running wild? Perhaps that's what those men had been hunting with their shotguns. But surely they would have warned her if she was in any danger.

The thought makes her shudder anyway, and she slides back down into the sleeping bag, draws it up over her head. A vision of sharp, bloodied teeth tearing flesh flashes across her mind. Alaska again – watching a wolf pack tear apart a caribou calf. She's getting carried away.

Start with the breath, remember. Count the inhale: one–two. Extend the out: one-two-three-four.

I am safe. I am safe. I am safe.

The howls come again, echoing through the dark like some cliché in a gothic horror.

Perhaps it's not real. Perhaps, just like the previous night, she's creating something out of nothing. Things sound different in the dark. Noise travels differently. It's probably the wind hitting the turbines. Yes. That must be it. That *must* be it.

A pressure builds in her chest. The compulsion to know, to understand, to create sense and certainty out of doubt and fear. There will be no sleep if she doesn't check.

She climbs out of the sleeping bag and squats by the door, listening. The howls have stopped, but now she picks out another sound close by – the scuffle of something moving about outside the tent. It turns her cold.

Suddenly aware of the flimsiness of the old nylon between her and the dark expanse of the moor, she has the urgent certainty that she's been watched. That she's prey. She fumbles for the lantern and clicks it on. If there is some animal out there, the light might scare it away. She tries to calm herself. What's most likely? A sheep, wandering and lost. A fox, curious at her human smells. She strains to hear more. The faint scattering of gravel, and a low, snorting breath.

She needs to know.

Forcing down the welling dread, she grabs her torch and flicks it on. Slowly, she unzips the tent's inner lining, then pauses, her hand on the outer zip, breath short and shuddering.

Come on. Stop being ridiculous.

Cautiously, she opens the tent flap and sends the torch beam out into the night.

Nothing.

Just the flat grey expanse of the turbine platform, the same as the night before. She crawls forward, the night air a cool balm, and scans left and right.

There's nothing to see. Just the turbine tower, glowing blue in the moonlight. A few stars blinking.

She takes a deep breath and lets it out slowly. Listens. The turbine generator hums, the blades whisper in their rhythmic dance.

There's nothing out here.

She's imagining things again. She must be.

Her heartbeat begins to slow.

She runs the torch beam in a semi-circle, skirting the edge of the platform toward the open moor, and up over the unnatural rise in the ground left behind by the construction crew. There, at the top of the slope, she sees two bright spots in the dark – the luminous white eyeshine of a wolf.

Day 3

Easting: 398085 Northing: 433506

She chooses a spot further from Turbine 34, where the detritus of construction is less likely to contaminate her results. She needs a place that wasn't disrupted by the building work, that hasn't been disturbed for years, since long before the windfarm was begun. She finds a promising patch of sphagnum, littered with the cheerful yellow blooms of bog asphodel and tormentil, like sprinkles on a cupcake. Though she's loath to uproot the pretty little plants, they're a sign that this spot is still nutrient rich, and therefore, a good candidate. She assesses the soil's density and moisture levels, then, satisfied, starts to dig.

She works there though the morning, chipping away the dried and compacted peat to reach damp under-layers, until the midday sun starts to bake her shoulders through the factor 50. She emerges from her ditch stinking like sewage, meaty with the stench of rotting dead things, her sample pots almost steaming with methane. She'd been right that the spot she'd chosen was virgin earth, but she's disappointed by the lack of progress and after another sleepless night, she's distracted. It's hard to focus, her mind wandering.

She can't stop thinking about the wolf-call, those incandescent canine eyes. It had been only a fleeting moment before the creature had turned and fled, a shadow shape in the moon's cast. A thrumming, primal fear as she'd frantically skimmed the torch's beam across the turbine platform, but there was nothing more.

Eventually, she had returned to the tent and tried to convince herself that it must have been a dog. *Must* have been. Can't have been anything else. A stray perhaps, or, more likely, someone's escaped pet, lost and calling for its owner. Setting off the other dogs at nearby farms. These things happen all the time. Perhaps she could find out who it belongs to and report the sighting.

Taking a break back at the tent, waiting for water to boil, she grabs the Ordnance Survey map and spreads it flat.

She charts the closest houses remembering which are renovated, which are derelict, and those farms still clinging on at the margins. It confirms what she already knows. The dwelling closest to her camp site is the one she's been avoiding. The old, ruined farmhouse at the high edge of the moor.

***

The first time they'd gone to the moortop, Kent had refused to pick her up at home.

'Remember what I said? Just you and me, right? No one else needs to know.'

He'd unfolded the map, spread it wide on the desk, the undulations of pen pots, staplers and Bunsen burners creating a miniature replica of the landscape laid out before them.

She'd followed the lane with a fingertip until the dotted line stopped at a tiny rectangle.

'Here. Meet me here.'

An abandoned farmhouse, about a mile from home, perched like a dead crow on a fence at the fringe of the moor. The only people who ever visited were farm lads who came to dump silage for the sheep and the occasional curious rambler.

He'd nodded, seeming pleased by her choice. But now he was late, and her body was livid with questions. Will he come? Does he like me? Should I have worn this dress?

Not that she minded waiting. It was early November, but winter hadn't yet gripped the hills. A low autumn sun attempted to break through the morning mist. As she'd paced the mile from home, skirting the edges of fields and clambering over dry-stone walls, she'd felt protected by this opaque cover, moving unseen through an insubstantial landscape, the weak sunlight tinting everything dandelion. The only creatures she saw were the nicotine-coloured sheep, who raised their heads, briefly curious, before returning to their ruminative chewing. She could count on them to keep her secret.

She and Cousin Jim had played here as children, before the roof caved in, daring each other to climb the rotten stairs and poke at spiders in cobwebby corners. The place had been a treasure trove of left-behind crockery, cracked oil lamps and rotting rag rugs. A reliquary for animal bones. Once, they'd found the decomposing corpse of a fox, curled in a cupboard. She'd nudged it with a stick, disturbing the feeding maggots, and Jim had chucked up in the old butler sink. Not long after, someone had cleared the remnants of human habitation, demolished the health hazard stairs and boarded the windows, but the old kitchen still had its ceiling, and a rusting stove that could still be lit. She and Jim used to feed it with peat cuttings from the old turbary field. She daydreamed that one day, when she was grown up and had money, she'd buy the place and turn it back into a home. Her father griped about incomers buying up the old properties, turning the old farming families off the land, but no one seemed to want this place.

At last, the headlights of Kent's ancient Volkswagen Beetle glowed dimly through the murk. The car see-sawed the last stretch, complaining of ill-treatment on the rutted track, and pulled up in front of the house with a rachet of the hand break. He jumped out of the car and flipped open the boot in one fluid movement, lifted out an old canvas backpack and slammed the door with a shotgun crack.

'Morning.'

He looked exactly as he always did. Doc Martens, black jeans, baggy black jumper. A khaki Army Surplus greatcoat. Thank God she'd gone with the dress and Docs, rather than the overalls and wellingtons she'd been considering. She hadn't wanted to look like she was trying too hard – or trying at all – but neither did she want to look like she'd just stepped out of the cow barn. She'd applied eyeliner and mascara, a slick of Rimmel Heather Shimmer, but wiped off the latter when she'd caught a glimpse of herself in the hallway mirror. Who was she kidding?

'Morning. Found it OK?' She could see the map spread out on the passenger seat.

'Took a couple of wrong turns – that's why I'm late. But it doesn't matter. I'm here now.' He glanced at the hulking ruin behind her. 'Quite a spot.'

'Yeah. No one really comes up this way.'

He stood, looking at the crumbling walls, the hollow watching windows. In a tree close by, a couple of magpies squabbled, their machine gun ak-ak bouncing off the old stone.

'Are you ready to go?' he asked, hitching the pack onto his back. 'I've got everything we need. I thought we could start with some basic observation, surveying, that sort of thing, then collect some samples to take back to the lab.'

'Sounds good.'

'Well then, lead the way. You're the local. I'm in your hands.'

The way he said it made her insides turn to liquid.

Observation, he'd said. So, she observed. Couldn't take her eyes off him. She noticed the way his cheeks flushed as he puffed his way uphill, relieving his usual pallor and making him look somehow younger, more boyish. She noticed how, when he pointed out some landscape feature, he would lean in close to match her eyeline, and she could smell him – old wool, tobacco and, very faintly, yesterday's sweat. An intoxicatingly male scent. She noticed too, how, when he held her gaze, one corner of his mouth would curl upward, as if he were amused by private thoughts.

They reached the moortop – the broad plateau of mature blanket bog they were there to investigate. The mist had lifted by now, and the sun was bright, golden autumnal light enriching the moor's palate of greens and browns, burgundies and purples. The odd patch of lilac heather still clinging on, and scorched swathes of grey where the keepers had been burning. Far off, a single slash of plasticky red screamed like a warning flag. Probably feed bags left behind by the estate staff.

He dropped the pack and shaded his eyes, taking it in.

'So, this is – what do they call it? Those women writers. The sisters. Wuthering Heights and all that?'

'The Brontës?'

'That's it. Brontë Country. Cathy and Heathcliff. Kate Bush. All those ghosts trying to climb in the windows ...' He made a scornful face, mimed tapping an imaginary windowpane.

She laughed. 'Not a fan?'

'Please, do I look like I read romances?'

'Well, Wuthering Heights in't really a romance...'

'All that wailing and gnashing of teeth? Sounds like a romance to me.'

'That's not really—'

'OK, I admit, I've never read it. Lady novelists...' He rolled his eyes.

With his shock of dark curls and billowing greatcoat, he could've been cast as Heathcliff himself but she kept the thought to herself.

'Right, lead on. Find me a likely spot away from the path. Mosses. Fungi. Peat. All that good Yorkshire stuff.' He shouldered the pack again and looked at her expectantly.

She scanned the moor, her gaze landing on the uncanny splash of red plastic. At least they should check that out. 'I hope you don't mind getting your feet wet.'

As they neared the object, she saw that it was a tent – or at least, the remains of one – clearly old, filthy and tattered as a shroud, pale plastic rods protruding like broken bones. No sign of anyone nearby, or anything you might expect to find if someone had simply abandoned their camping spot, though why anyone would pitch a tent up here was beyond her. The colour seemed incongruously garish. The way the rods, lying fractured and disjointed, still woven through the tent's flysheet, reminded her of a carcass she once saw. A dead sheep – one of theirs – that had lain undisturbed for days. By the time Dad had brought it back from the high fell, half its innards had been devoured, a great scarlet gash where its belly should've been, the dome of ribs, its eyes sightless black holes.

Neither of them spoke.

A cold shiver of distaste slid down her spine.

He was the one to investigate, bending to look inside, and toeing the broken poles, though it was obvious no one had been here for months. It was strange she'd not noticed it before. Strange the keepers hadn't moved it. But then, people left all kinds of weird shit lying around the countryside. Once, she and Jim had found a 1940s bicycle dumped in a clough, complete with wicker basket still fastened to the front handlebars. They'd hauled it out, Jim had fixed it up and ridden it for years, swearing stubbornly that it dealt perfectly well with the hills. Once, they'd found a whole car bonnet in woodland, miles from anywhere. And the old fridges and washing machines and mattresses, fly-tipped in their fields as if dropped overnight by UFO, were regular as roadkill. On the scale of weirdness, this was barely worth noting.

She told him so, and he looked at her with a mixture of fascination and disbelief. She told him about some of the things she'd found, and he laughed and bumped shoulders with her. He thought she was making it up. She wasn't, but if he wanted to think so, fine. Anything to make him look at her like that.

Lunch was ham and cucumber sandwiches. No butter, so the bread was soggy. A flask of weak, sweet tea. Flapjacks from the Cooperative. She didn't eat much. She was too full. Full of him – his every move, every look, every touch. And he did touch her. Fingers grazed as he passed her the flask, knees collided as they knelt to collect samples, a hand offered to help her across a dyke. Each touch imprinting on her skin as if he were branding her, claiming her, marking her out like the raddled tups in the fields. Each time a thrill. A question.

By the time they returned to the car, the light was beginning to fade and the temperature dropping. Her fingers were numbed and clumsy, but still, she didn't want the day to end.

He opened the boot and carefully arranged the backpack, now stacked with neatly filled and labelled sample dishes.

'I can give you a lift back to the road,' he said. 'But I'll have to drop you there.'

They couldn't be seen together. Mustn't drive through town. She understood.

'Here, put your stuff in the back.'

He took the small knapsack from her, catching her fingers. 'My God, you're freezing. Your fingers are practically blue.'

He cradled her hands in his, rubbed them gently, brought them to his mouth and exhaled a hot, damp breath, sending her spiralling.

A moment of hesitation.

She would look back later and realise – *that* was the moment, the point of no return for them both, but she will never be sure who moved first, because her memory glitches. She recalls her hands in his, his hot breath, and looking over his shoulder toward the windows of the ruined farmhouse, suddenly struck by a foreboding sense that they were watched. And then, his tongue is in her mouth, and she is pressed up against the car, the cold, unrelenting steel against her back. He'd tasted of the rollies he'd smoked, and the sweet, sugared tea. He'd pushed against her urgently, hard against her hip, hands finding their way beneath her coat to pull her closer still. She could have moved away, could have stopped it then, but she didn't want to. She wanted him, more than anything. She'll look back and know – that was the moment he made her his.

The old path is completely overgrown, almost invisible, though it's still marked on the GPS. A tiny, dotted line winding along the side of the moor and down the hillside, jack-knifing to avoid what used to be a dyke. The dyke has long dried up, and the only creatures that still use this route are the straying sheep. She follows it by memory, her feet finding their way, until she sees the old ruin, tucked against the slope of the fell.

Except it isn't a ruin anymore.

The house's blackened gritstone face has been sand-blasted to a buttery beige and skylights glint in the grey slate of a new roof. Terracotta chimney pots adorn the rebuilt stacks. Where the building's windows had once glowered, new triple-glazing blinks innocently back, framed in tasteful Farrow & Ball. A heat pump sits where the old lean-to used to be, and on the far side, a double height garage has replaced the impenetrable tangle of pallets and chicken wire that had once served as a coop. A spotless Range Rover squats outside like a fat shining stag beetle, a black cable leading to a charging point on the wall.

In the yard, the old sets have been restored and lev-elled, and a paved path leads to a neat, fenced rec-tangle of lawn, surrounded by wilting flower beds. Waist-height nettles encroach at the borders, and a few mole hills threaten to ruin the illusion of perfection, but there's the cheerful blue plastic of a trampoline, a greenhouse glinting in the sun, tomatoes ripening. The place looks prosperous. Happy.

For a moment she thinks she's got it wrong – this is the wrong house. But no. There's the big stone lintel over the kitchen window with the witch mark hatched into one corner, and there's the old outhouse, rebuilt, a twee hand-painted sign reading 'Potting Shed' over the door.

As she takes it in, a sudden hatchet of anger lodges itself in her chest. This house was supposed to be hers, and now they've spoiled it. They've taken away all the things she loved about it. She stops herself from charging down the hill, knocking at the front door and demanding answers. They can't help her. She knows that. She's being unreasonable.

She's about to force herself away when a side door opens and a small red dot of a child comes out of the house and runs to the withered patch of green lawn, followed by a dog.

A dog! A mid-sized mutt. A rescue, no doubt, and capable of howling like a goddamn wolf. Probably. Could it be the creature she saw in the night? It's possible, though her instinct says otherwise.

And the boy. Red shirt and shorts. Some sort of football kit. He climbs onto the trampoline and starts bouncing. She can hear him singing some silly jingle she doesn't recognise.

She feels an incredible swell of resentment toward this boy and his dog, all benevolent intentions forgotten.

Where is the tumbledown ruin she once loved? What have they done to this place that has been a fixture in the story of her life. Whenever she thinks of those days, it's always to this place that she returns. She remembers every nook and cranny, every cobwebby corner, every cold, unlovely stone, as if she is connected, somehow anchored here. To see that child so oblivious, so care-free, makes her sick with envy, and something else, a strange sense of disintegration, as if something impor-tant has been destroyed. As if something inside her is falling apart, tumbling to ruin, like the old gritstone walls used to be.

She shouldn't have come.

She turns away and starts the climb back up to the camp. Around her, the hum of the turbines rises, like a swarm of electrical bees.

Day 4

Dawn comes early this time of year. As the sky pales, she pulls herself from heavy sleep – the blank, dreamless sleep of exhaustion – with a sense of relief. No strange noises in the night. No anguished, lingering dread. No sickly hangover from bad dreams. In the grey fugue of first light, the tent's inner is desaturated, a sepia plate, and all is calm.

She'd needed a decent rest. Her visit to the old farm had triggered a cascade of memories and she'd spent the evening perched at the mouth of the tent, watching the meditative rotation of the monolithic turbine, questioning everything – her choices, her beliefs, the veracity of her own story – until, spent, she'd crawled into the sleeping bag and drifted off.

A new day brings new perspective, and as she flicks on the lantern, she decides to put all that behind her.

She's here for a reason. She's close – she can feel it. Maybe today she'll find what she's looking for.

It's much cooler this morning. There's not much wind, but Turbine 34 turns, its whirring industrial cacophony seeming loud in the quiet of first light. Distant birdcall sounds from somewhere on the wooded valley slopes, at odds with a mechanical tumult of clatters and bangs. It must be the other turbines, the valley acting as an echo chamber now the wind has dropped. That's probably what woke her.

She climbs out of the sleeping bag and pulls on a jumper. It's not cold exactly, but the thick, pressing heat has broken – the first sign that a change is coming.

Outside, wisps of early morning mist puddle round her ankles like dry ice. The moor is wreathed in it, the high plateau an island. In the valleys, thick clouds sit like cotton wool. Cloud inversion is rare at this time of year – usually reserved for chilly autumn mornings – but that's what reveals itself as the sky brightens. Perhaps it is this low cloud, sitting in the hollows and cloughs, that causes sound to carry differently. She can hear the distinct chink-clunk of metal-on-metal travelling up from the valley floor. The hum of early-morning activity, hidden by nature's veil. The clatter of machinery, roadworks perhaps, or some kind of construction. Behind her, Turbine 34 hums.

From her viewpoint, she can see one of the old chimneys that dot the valley bottom, belonging to the mills that once dominated, peeking through the cloud blanket, a grey gritstone silhouette. A puff of cloud stretches from its mouth into the brightening sky, creating the illusion of smoke. A few hundred feet along the valley floor, another chimney, the same strange plume erupting from its mouth.

She blinks, rubs her tired eyes, then fetches her camera, keen to capture this hallucination of the area's industrial heyday, these valleys as the cradle of capitalism. She imagines the photo, mounted and framed in a gallery somewhere. What would she call it? *Resurrection. 19th Century Morning. Ruins Reborn*. She points the camera. Shoots. Checks the image on the digital screen. There's the valley, the cloud settling between wooded steeps. The sky, a pale blue.

No chimneys.

She frowns, glances at the view before her, back at the screen. The images do not match. A sudden, violent surge of nausea makes her reel and for a moment she doubles over, hands on knees, breathing through it, the camera dangling loose around her neck.

Glancing up, she can see that it's no illusion – both chimneys emit lazy columns of smutted smoke that float above the cloud and diffuse into the dawn sky.

She breathes slow and steady until she's ready to stand. Then, slowly, she clambers up the spoil heap to one side of her camp – the highest point possible – and gains a clearer view of the valley, curving off into the distance. There is another chimney beyond the second, and another. A whole line of them. Proud stone sentinels of a disappeared world, blackened by soot and weather.

This can't be right. She knows those chimneys aren't there. The mills they once belonged to are long gone, torn down, derelict, or turned into offices and apartments, the chimneys deemed unsafe and dismantled, brick by brick.

Her mind stutters, unable to make sense of what she's seeing. New sounds reach her – not, she realises now, the electrical hum and whir of the turbines, but the hiss and burble of steam, the clatter of looms, the sudden toll of factory bells. She picks out each sound like a morsel, a delicacy, above the hum.

Her head begins to thump, a sharp needle stabbing behind her right eye. Her vision tilts and shimmers at the periphery. Is she dreaming? She *must* be dreaming. She had been so upset yesterday, so fixated on things best forgotten, that this vision of the valley's industrial past has crept into her consciousness. She looks at her arms, pale and mottled in the morning light, the scars and wrinkles on her hands, rocked by a disorientating sense that she can't trust herself, can't believe her senses. She counts the moles on her left wrist. One. Two. Three. She shuts her eyes and concentrates on the dull throb of her sore ankle, the blood-beat coursing in her veins.

When she opens them, nothing has changed. The chimneys are still there, a gathering of crow-black sentries, belching their waste breath, a message to the heavens. She realises, it's not cloud in the valley – it's smog, the thick yellowish belch of industry, waiting for the sun to burn it off.

Back in the tent she rummages for her binoculars. They are real, even if what she sees is not. Her heart patters irregularly. Doctor Kagehira's voice comes to mind – *remember your breathing* – but she has no time for that now.

Out of the tent and back up the spoil heap to get the best view, ignoring the pain as she stumbles and her ankle tweaks.

It's obvious before she focuses the Nikons – the chimneys are gone. Where the dark brotherhood had stood, nothing. Just the dissipating remains of morning mist. The outline of homes and warehouses. The railway track, a caterpillar outline of an early commuter train. She scans the valley, finds the single chimney that she knows still stands. It's clear of smoke, its clean, sandblasted lip glowing gold in the first rays of morning sunrise.

Nearby, a single lark rises from the heather.

The wooden handle of the trowel feels familiar and comforting, worn contours fitting perfectly in her hand. There's better equipment available these days – smaller, lighter, articulated, folding into neat little boxes for transportation – but she's never been able to let this one go. It had been a gift on her eighteenth birthday, a talisman for the life to come, the life she was now expected to have. It was a sign, she knew, that her parents had accepted her choice, and if she got the results she needed, she would be leaving in the autumn.

The gifts had been waiting for her in the kitchen on the morning of her birthday, next to a cooling plate of eggs and bacon: the trowel, a good set of waterproofs and a tent, the best they could afford from Millets, with a built-in groundsheet and a bright red outer.

'For your field trips,' Mum had said, beaming.

'Built to last,' added Dad, handling the trowel approvingly. 'Sheffield Steel – last you a lifetime.'

Jim had scoffed. For his eighteenth he'd got a rusting Ford Fiesta in which a rotation of local barmaids then spent their Saturday nights. But she knew this was her parents' way of telling her she was forgiven, that they had come around. That they were, perhaps, even proud of her and what she might become.

The college open evening had been the turning point. Kent's charm and effusive praise, the way he'd flattered them, placing credit for her successes in their parenting, just the right side of obsequious. He had opened their eyes in a way she'd failed to do, speaking enthusiastically of academic accolades, of a bright, lucrative future, while she squirmed, tortured by a heady mixture of embarrassment and lust. The plastic chair sticking to her bare legs.

The steel edge of the trowel is still sound – Dad was right – but now she struggles with the dried compacted peat. She's chosen this spot as an example of peat deterioration. The problems are obvious at ground level, the surface naked of vegetation except a few tenacious outcrops of lichen and heather, the wet-loving grasses failing to get a foothold. The peat is hard and cracked, deep fissures creating a miniature landscape of ravines and crevices. She needs to know how deep these fissures go. If they are as bad as she suspects, then the lower layers of peat will dry out and release the carbon dioxide they store. If they reach bedrock, then it's possible for the entire blanket bog to destabilise.

She works slowly and conscientiously. At first, it's soothing and she soon loses herself in the familiarity of process, buries herself in the task. Fastidiously, she collects her samples, placing each in a Petrie dish, labelling it, slowly building a little stack beside her. The same as always.

The upper layers of peat crumble to dust between her fingers. She knows that if she looks at these samples through the microscope, she'll see what she's afraid of. That the peat is dead. That what was – and should be – a complete ecosystem, brimming with life, is now a wasteland. A desert, unable to sustain the creatures it depends upon. A vicious cycle of destruction.

Carefully, she works her way down the face of one fissure, keen to explore its depths, to assess the impact of the baking summer heat and drought, the unintended consequences of the wind farm's construction, the way the natural water table has been disrupted, the possibility that electrical vibrations might disturb this mysterious underworld. It's worse than she anticipated, the peat parched almost a foot down before she reaches moisture.

It would take three hundred years to lay down a foot of peat – it has taken fewer than ten to destroy it.

She kneels back, sucks in the warm air, filling her lungs with the earthy, rotten scent her digging has released. It's not her job to judge, she reminds herself, but to observe, to monitor and record, dispassionately if she can. She hears the voices of her university lecturers, her bosses over the years. A scientist must be able to divorce from emotion – to rise above such human reaction to see things as they are, not as they seem. To question. To reason.

It is enlightenment thinking. The rationale of rich, white men who had forgotten what it was like to have your hands in the soil, to live with and in the natural world, to learn from it and not about it. She had worked by their creed for three decades before even questioning it, forgetting – denying – the lessons learned young, those the moor had taught her.

She doesn't want to think about the things she's seen these last few days, the uncanny sense of dislocation as if her grip on reality is slipping, the otherworldly, forbidding sense of something pressing at her consciousness, just out of sight. But questions plague her anyway and images force themselves forward, making her throat tighten, making her breathless: those hostile, odd-looking men with their gundogs; those hungry canine eyes, luminous in the black night; the unexplainable hallucinations of the morning. She can't explain *that* away. It's as if, now she's here alone, after all these years, the moor is revealing things she'd rather not know. Or else, she's losing her mind.

She shakes off the questions and submerses herself in the task at hand, the pit around her deepening gradually, until she's a metre down in the ancient peat, lulled by the familiar cosseting smell. The stink of rot, notes of mushroom and smoke, bog wood and flint and stone. The warm, woody musk of heather bloom. She breathes it in, lets it soothe her, lets the earth work its magic.

She is absorbed, mining carefully around the pale roots of a heather plant, curious about the colonies of microorganisms that might support its growth. She forgets to eat, to drink, does not notice the pressing heat of midday soften to late afternoon, does not notice the temperature drop, or the clouds that begin to collect on the eastern horizon. The stack of sample pots teeters above the rim of the pit. Her focus is total. This, she can understand. This, she can control.

The light is harvest-gold by the time the peat reveals something unexpected. Captured by the straggling, deepest roots of the heather she finds an object. Pale and hard, but not stone, and not the chunks of concrete that have plagued her. Carefully, she excavates, exposing a slim stretch of yellowed bone.

Animal, perhaps. Or something else. She's not sure.

She's no stranger to dead things on the moor. Her childhood had been peppered with macabre finds: crows hung on fences as warnings, swollen lamb carcasses, and once, a stag, freshly dead with eyes still intact. By the time she and Jim had tugged the trolley up the track – a race to beat the keepers – the eyes were already gone, jackdaws pecking at the sockets. Jim had the antlers mounted on his wall for years, a trophy, as if he had shot it himself.

She tries to calm her excitement, patiently scraping away the black peat to reveal a length of bone with the bulbous protuberance of a joint at either end. The heather has grown around it, roots cradling it, creating the illusion of veins on the bone's surface. She works to gently untether it, superstitious suddenly about damaging the plant above. Her world shrinks to this patch of earth, until she has cleared enough to loosen her find.

Tentatively she levers it from its long resting place.

It is stained brown, about the length of a school ruler. At one end the rounded head of a ball joint, the tubercle slimming to a long, elegant length, then the splayed trochlea. She's no anatomist but the words come back to her like poetry: radial fossa, capitulum, deltoid ridge.

She wipes it clean, turns it about, then holds it gently against her upper arm. Yes, she's right. Human. A humerus bone. She slots it against her own, from shoulder to elbow.

It fits perfectly.

The first time she'd seen him angry was the day of the flat tyre.

She was waiting at the old ruin. January cold nipped through the knitted-by-Nan mittens that had been a Christmas gift. She hated them, of course, but it was too cold for vanity. She wasn't even sure he'd come. Not sure the Beetle would make it down the icy track. She shivered in the doorway, fretting at a snagged thread on her scarf, imagining the car in a ditch.

The letter had come three days ago, but she'd told no one, not even Sally. She wanted him to be the first to know.

At last, she spied exhaust fumes coughing up the track and soon he pulled up with the usual screech of the handbrake. He was dressed in his khaki greatcoat, collar flipped, black leather gloves and a thin black scarf the only concession to the freezing temperatures of deep winter. Breath snaked about his head, eyes sharp and glittery. God, he was beautiful. She pulled off the mittens and shoved them into a pocket.

His mouth tasted of cigarettes and chewing gum and a faint yeasty taint of Weetabix. He took off his own gloves and burrowed cold fingers beneath her thermals. He smelled so good. Old wool and Radox. The blue one.

The Christmas holidays had been torture. Three weeks of moping about the farm, roped into cleaning out cowsheds and prepping the barn for lambing. Then, college again, pretending to concentrate on lessons when all she'd wanted was to reach out and touch him.

She had to admit there was something delicious about their shared secret. A kind of intoxicating pleasure in his cool glances. Euphoria in the knowledge of what they'd done. What they would do again.

She hadn't told a soul. Somehow, she'd kept this volcano of feeling from erupting, even though some days, her desire seemed like a separate entity, a creature, eating her alive. It hurt, this fleshly thing, that sustained and destroyed her all at once.

She understood why it had to be this way. What was at stake. His job, for one. His future. Hers, too. Theirs. Together.

And now, one more secret. She couldn't hold it back any longer.

She broke away, drew the letter from the depths of her layers. 'Read this.'

He released her and unfolded the single sheaf. There it was, balanced in the air between them – the college's embossed crest, the simple words in Times New Roman. It was like a mythical text, a grimoire, possessing the power of transformation.

His eyes widened. Darkened.

'Well done. I always said you could do it.' His teacher voice.

'It's only an offer.'

He scanned the letter again, frowning. She could see him thinking, assessing. 'It's a good, solid offer. You'll get these grades, if you work hard.' She couldn't read his tone. This wasn't how she'd imagined his reaction.

'Aren't you pleased?'

'Yes ... yes, of course I am.' He pulled her close, crushing the letter between them, cradled her face with his free hand. 'I missed you, that's all.'

'I missed you, too. So much.' To her horror, she felt tears spring, but he seemed to like it.

There was frost on the pile of blankets she'd carried from home, ferreted from the back of the airing cupboard over the weeks. The old camping mat, crisp with cold. Little icicles dangling from the beams in the old kitchen. Their bed looked like a vagrant's den, an animal's nest. She didn't care. Didn't notice the chill as he pushed her down and tugged at her leggings. She hadn't worn underwear and was glad of it as he looked up at her from between her thighs, eyes voracious. He'd flipped her over and pulled her up onto her knees, flattening her palms against damp, cold stone.

An hour later, they stumbled out into fading afternoon light to find the Beetle had a flat.

He crouched and peered at it. A nail head protruded from the rubber, almost mocking in its obviousness. 'Fuck.'

He straightened with a hard scowl. 'Fucking great.'

'It's just a flat.'

He didn't seem to hear her. He paced away, swearing, then returned and kicked at the wheel hub – *Fuck. Shit. Fuck*. The angles of his face grew sharp and mask-like. Spittle flew from the corner of his mouth. Then, he spun about and dug in a pocket for tobacco.

She stood, silent and shocked, while he rolled a fag, muttering under his breath. She'd never seen him angry. The change so swift he seemed to spark with it. Eyes like chips of flint. It made her feel strange inside.

He ignored her, lit the cigarette, took a long draw and went back for another violent boot of the car tyre – *Piece. Of. Shit.*

'We can fix it,' she tried. 'If you have a spare?'

He hacked out a bitter laugh. 'Why would *I* know how to do *that*?'

'Er ... 'cause you own a car?' She felt him withdraw immediately – felt it physically – like the sudden removal of a warm blanket, leaving her exposed and chilled. Shit. She'd fucked up.

He threw her a look of contempt. 'And you do, I suppose. You must do things like that all the time *on the farm.*'

Why was he behaving like this? Taking it out on her? He'd never spoken to her that way before. It wasn't her fault. She ignored the niggling little warning voice that rose in her core. She needed to soothe him. Make it better. Make everything alright again.

'Please, let me help.'

He gave an exasperated sigh and chucked the keys in her direction. They landed with a bell-like tinkle at her feet. 'Oh, for fuck's sake. Under the bonnet.'

By the time she was done, her fingers were numb and blackened with grease and dirt, but for once she was grateful to Dad for the practicality he'd instilled in her. She hefted the flat into the space left behind by the spare, slammed the bonnet and walked over to where he was perched on a fallen lintel, chain smoking and glowering.

'OK. All done. That should get you home. Or to a garage, at least.'

He was calmer now, a little sheepish. 'Sorry about all that. Come here.' He enfolded her inside his greatcoat. She made herself small, snuggled against his chest. The warmth, the scent of his skin, of sex. The knot in her solar plexus evaporated. It was just a stupid flat tyre. Nothing more. Nothing to get upset about.

As she climbed the track toward home, she recalled a conversation she'd had with Sally back in December. It had been the day of her interview at Oxford and Sally had met her from the train. Over cheap drinks in The Fox, she'd recounted every detail of the day, describing the golden stone buildings of the city, the bicycling students, the bearded and bowtied professor who'd interviewed her. Her friend listened, stifling yawns.

Two pints in and Sally spoke up. 'But seriously, d'you think you'd be happy at a place like that?'

'Why not?'

'In't it full of private school knobheads? In't they all stuck up arseholes?'

'Nah. They take all sorts these days. Look at Kent.'

'Kent?'

'Yeah. He went there and turned out alright.'

Sally scrunched her face in the way she did when she clearly had an opinion to share. 'Yer think?'

'I know you think he's posh, but he's a decent bloke.'

Sally made a disbelieving fart sound.

'He *is*,' she insisted. 'You just don't know him.'

'And you do?' Sally cocked a sceptical brow. 'Anyway, he's a fraud. A bullshitter. Oxford, my arse.'

'What do you mean?'

'He got kicked out. You know that, right?'

'What?'

'He got kicked out of Oxford.'

'Bollocks. Who says?'

'Kevin's mum.' Kevin, Sally's on-again, off-again boyfriend, and his mum, always sticking her nose where it wasn't wanted.

'What the fuck does *she* know?'

'Hey, don't shoot the messenger. I'm just telling you what she said. Apparently Kent almost got fired last term because they found out he'd lied on his CV. He got kicked out of Oxford. Big mystery why – no one seems to know. Kevin reckons on a scandal, but it were probably just for being an arrogant twat.' Sally smirked, clearly enjoying herself. 'He ended up at one of the old polys. In disgrace.'

'Sounds like bullshit to me.'

She thought of all the stories of Oxford Kent had shared. All the places he'd described, the lecturers, the names he'd dropped – names she recognised from articles in *The Lancet*.

'Maybe, but think on it – if he's got a first-class degree from Oxford, like he said, why is he teaching us in a shitty sixth form college?'

'If it *was* true, they'd have fired him.'

'I dunno – they're so desperate for teachers. He probably talked 'em round. Why are you defending him anyway?' Sally elbowed her. 'Has someone got a crush?'

For a moment, she'd been tempted to spill, just to watch Sally's face. But she couldn't. She'd promised him so many times – to tell would've been betrayal.

She forced a laugh. 'As if…'

She could've asked him about the rumours, of course, but she knew what he'd say – *Don't you trust me?* – and couldn't bear the hurt look in his eyes, couldn't risk jeopardising things. Still, Sally's revelation made her uneasy, a small seed of doubt rooting deep. But he wouldn't lie to her, she reassured herself. He wouldn't do that. They had something special – he'd said so himself. Precious. Sacred. Private. Those beautiful words he'd used that she carried with her like talismans. It was his belief in her that had secured the letter in her pocket, and the possibility of the bright future that now lay before her, shimmering like a mirage. She owed him. She needed him. She loved him. That couldn't all be based on lies. Could it?

Night

She dreams again.

She wakes – as usual – with breath-stealing pressure at her throat, the earth closing above her, filling her mouth, grit and rust and smoke on her tongue, turning everything black.

Her fingers fumble for the lantern's switch and the tent floods with brothel-red light. Remember your breath. Count the inhale: one–two. Extend the out: one-two-three-four.

I am safe. I am safe. I am safe.

As she calms, she becomes aware of a new resonance. The wind has picked up, but it sounds different. She concentrates. Listens. She can't hear Turbine 34. She can't hear any of the turbines at all.

She's become so accustomed to the constant electrical drone, the background squeals and clicks and clunks of gears and transformers, that it has begun to blend with the wilder soundscape of the moor. Now, what reaches her is not the steady whoosh of rotating turbine blades, but a sound just as familiar – the rustle of breeze through treetops.

She holds her breath, convinced it's the echo of her own unsteady exhalation, a hangover from the dream, but no – it's still there. It must be an auditory hallucination, caused perhaps by a change in atmospheric pressure or wind direction. But then, another noise – human this time – a shout.

Oh, shit. Not again.

She lies there a minute more, then crawls out of the sleeping bag and finds her torch. If there are people out there, she can't have them walking all over the site, messing things up, tripping over quadrats and flag markers, falling into the pit she'd left exposed. She checks the time: 3.32 a.m. *Who the fuck is out there at this hour, and what are they doing?*

She pauses, straining to hear more. Maybe she's imagining things again. No – the distinct sound of a raised male voice reaches her. Could it be the gamekeepers? Those men she'd seen with the dogs. There's no earthly reason for them to be up here now. There must be something else going on. Old memories of police searches and missing girls flit through her mind, though she can't hear sirens, or the beat of helicopter blades, or anything that suggests such predictable horrors. It's probably just some pissed up village lads, or

protestors, come to spray paint profanities on the turbines.

She unzips the tent's inner, then the fly, and points
the torch beam out into the dark. The light hits an
object about twelve feet away, and her heart stutters in
shock. She blinks, shakes herself, flicks the torch off and
on again, as if what she sees is an illusion caused by a
faulty battery. It's still there, silent and utterly indiffer-
ent to her disbelief – a tree.

Scanning the torch left and right, incredulity rising, she sees more. Full-grown specimens and younger
saplings, bark strangely bleached and desaturated to a
monotone grey in the bright LED light.

She clambers out and stands, barefoot, trying to
make sense of what her eyes tell her. The ground is
no longer the compacted sand and gravel of the turbine platform, but soft and yielding, littered with leaves
and ferns. Above, a tangled canopy of branches rustles
with verdant summer growth. Birch, rowan and willow.
Alder, ash and elm. A single oak, with gnarled limbs
bigger than any she's seen before.

Dreaming. She must be. She shuts her eyes, digs her
nails into her palms, breathes through the rising panic.

One–two. One-two-three-four.

I am safe. I am safe. I am safe.

When she opens them again, nothing has changed.

The sound of human voices comes again, raised above the hush of wind. This time, it sounds like singing, but it's barely a tune, more a low undulant humming, discordant and uncanny. Her confusion shifts to alarm, animal fear making her lungs contract, her breath shorten. She clicks off the torch. A wall of darkness falls. Where before, the night-time horizon was dotted with the far glittering lights of civilisation, lit by a fat summer moon, there is nothing but thick, absolute blackness. There is no horizon, no starlit sky, just the dense blanket of the overstory. Except, away to the east, a flicker of flame, glimpsed through the trees.

Her body tells her to hide. She flicks the torch back on and turns to the tent – her only protection – but the tent is gone. Where it had stood, just a small flattening of leaf-strewn ground.

Her head swims. This isn't possible.

She looks back toward the firelight and detects the movement of figures. Understanding fractures. She can't make sense of this. She can't explain this away.

Swallowing down her instincts, she steps toward the light, ignoring the scratch of forest litter on bare soles. Hesitantly, she runs fingertips over the ragged bark of the first tree she reaches. The old, broad oak. She half-expects it to be insubstantial – an apparition – and for her fingers to move through it, but the trunk is hard and unyielding, pulsing with gentle vitality that feels so familiar, so real. It should be reassuring, but it's not – it's horrifying – and she snatches her hand away.

Collecting her courage, she makes her way slowly toward the light, pushing through bracken and tangled low branches, disturbing some small creature that scurries away through the leaf fall. The hum of voices intensifies, rising and falling, rising and falling, a strange, wave-like incantation.

The trees around her begin to thin and she can see figures now, gathered in a clearing, illuminated by a bonfire. She turns off her torch, but grips it hard, afraid that if she puts it down it'll disappear, too. She creeps as close as she dares and squats behind a fallen ash, its upturned root bed offering camouflage. The earthy, woody scent of her hiding place melds with smoke from the bonfire, which has a strange, herbal taint – something pungent she doesn't recognise.

From here, she can see that this is a natural birch grove, a few stumps at the margins revealing where other trees have been felled to expand it, boundaries marked out by sharpened birchwood stakes and flickering fire torches, driven into the ground at intervals.

The singing – if it can be described as that – is coming from a group of men. She counts thirteen of them, all shaggy-haired and bearded, young and old, standing in a loose semi-circle. They'd look like a bunch of festival-destined tree-huggers, except they're all dressed in various shades of mud-coloured cloth and leather. A few wear sashes across bared chests, pinned with glinting metal broaches. She catches the shine of a blade as one man turns; a dagger's hilt thrust beneath a leather strap.

Opposite, a group of feral women, similarly bedraggle-haired and dressed in the same muted cloth, are huddled, crouching and swaying as one to the intonation of the men. Their long skirts are belted with twine, crude beads and pendants dangle in their hair and about their necks.

At the centre of the clearing stands a large wooden construction – a square frame with two cross struts making a central X, decorated with switches of willow and ivy and threaded with wildflowers: the deep purple of harebells and devil's-bit, the bright gold of rock rose, sprigs of blood-red rowan berries. A weird otherworldly atmosphere pervades like the bonfire's smoke.

She's heard the stories of course, of the cults and sects that have come here over the years, the witches, druids and satanists. Countless New Age pagans and occultists, the outcasts and drifters who would turn up, sleeping in caravans and begging change outside the Post Office. The steep wooded cloughs and barren moors are perfect for those looking for a discreet place where their bizarre rituals won't draw attention, but she'd never really believed it, never seen anything to back up the rumours of orgiastic bacchanalia that would occasionally scatter around the schoolyard or occupy bored pub regulars on a Friday night.

But the members of this strange collective don't seem like those folk. They don't seem ordinary at all. The way these people move is different. The sound they make is like nothing she's heard before. She sees no giveaways – no Crocs or Nikes, no pin-up girl tattoos, no telltale glow of a mobile. They seem whole. Real. Entirely present and part of this place.

A thought builds, a wave of recognition that she resists at first, a pressure buzzing at the corners of her consciousness like an angry wasp. Alternative words come back to her. Romantic words her father had spoken, spinning yarns over his whisky at the kitchen table, stories she had dismissed as the ramblings of old folk: Celts. Brigantes. The kingdom of Elmet. 'Our ancestors,' he would say, banging his fist on the worn oak and making the cutlery rattle. 'Our forefathers. Our sort 'ave been in these 'ills longer than tha knows.'

Now, the women begin to unpeel from their huddle, revealing faces daubed and streaked with reddish clay and, at the centre, a girl, squatting naked. Her hair is long and dark, falling in shining hanks. Slowly, she stands, aided by the women. She's young, bone thin, unmarked by childbirth or accident, the curve of her hips smooth and narrow, the pink nubs of her breasts upturned, the thatch between her legs stark against pale skin. There is something achingly familiar about her. She's trembling but expressionless as she spreads her arms and allows the women to dip their hands into a cauldron at her feet and anoint her with the same red loamy paint they wear. They are gentle with her, hands smoothing over hips and belly, shoulders and legs, until she is covered, all except her face. Her face, they leave bare.

When they are done, two of the women remain with the girl, while the others spread out, creating a half-moon opposite the men, completing the circle around the wooden frame. They join the chant, voices coming together, weaving and rising, sonorously beautiful.

Hidden behind the fallen ash tree, she is transfixed. The whole scene is dreamlike and vague, like a long-forgotten memory resurfacing, translated through a prism of illusion. She keeps expecting to wake, but as she watches, a new sensation overtakes her. She is lulled by the hypnotic song, by the heady smoke-scent. The boundaries of her body seem thinner somehow, her edges indistinct, permeable, as if she might gradually dissolve into the night air. As if parts of her might drift into the treetops and settle on the leaves like moths, and others meld with the soil, root deep into the damp earth with the badgers and moles. As if the people in the clearing are whole and tangible, and she is the one who is unreal, nothing but shadow and light.

Now, the two women with the girl are helping her drink from a small wooden cup. When she has done this, the girl steps toward the centre of the circle, toward the wooden frame, body glistening. She seems calm, lips moving in silent prayer. She stumbles and sways a little, as if she's drunk; the women catch her. They guide her as she turns, leans back against the frame and stretches her arms wide, limbs splayed against the spokes. The women bind her wrists and ankles, loop twine around her waist, securing her to the frame, as her head begins to droop.

The chanting rises a pitch, becomes edged with menace. Still hidden, she senses a sudden tension, sees how the men's bodies grow taught and expectant. Unease shifts deep in her centre, but the girl seems calm enough, her eyes closed, drowsy and nodding. They must have drugged her.

When the girl is secured, the two women step back and join the circle. The chanting grows louder, more insistent – becoming a calling out, a beckoning. The wind in the canopy seems to respond, shaking leaves like confetti.

Now, a figure emerges from the trees at the far side of the clearing. This man – it must be a man judging by his height and breadth – wears a mask. The pale bone of a large ram's skull, with black, empty eye sockets, two curled horns rising from the head plate. A long loose tunic and a pendant made of bones. She recognises the distinct butterflied shape of human vertebrae.

She sees the way the others revere this man, the power he holds, and she knows then, what will happen next. Sudden panic claws her from the inside.

The tethered girl sees him too and struggles weakly against her binds. As he enters the circle and moves toward her, she lets out a cry. She twists and kicks, head lolling drunkenly as she tries to free herself. He moves close, fixes her with the stare of those hollow, sightless eyes, and she falls silent again, frightened into submission. Her eyes roll white and her body goes limp.

She has seen animals behave like this at slaughter – terror as they understand their fate, the desperate fight for life, and then the horrid acceptance as they give in.

She should stop this. She should do something. But she doesn't. She can't. She can't move. Her limbs feel weak and insubstantial, her body pulsing with fragmented energy, as if parts of her are scattered and she is no longer whole. Her vision blurs, crystalising into a kaleidoscope of images. She is in the treetops, looking down. She is with the swaying women, part of their circle. She is behind the bone mask. She is bound tight to the frame. She is everywhere and nowhere, all at once. She is woven in their web, caught in invisible binds, spellbound as the horned man takes out a thin leather strap and steps behind the frame, comes up close behind the nodding girl.

She wants to close her eyes, wants to block out the droning song, but she can't even do that, can't switch off the succession of images that tumble like a sickening montage.

Abruptly, the chanting stops. There is nothing but the rising wind whispering in the canopy and the staggered breath of the tethered girl, loud and internal, as if it's her own.

The horned man takes hold of the girl's hair and pulls it back, exposing her throat. He slips the leather strap deftly around her neck. Her eyes open wide, as if in that moment, everything is revealed to her – all the world's beauty and all the world's horror.

Then, he pulls the strap tight.

As the girl's body fights for life, a pressing sensation builds at her own throat. A sharp point of pain at her windpipe. A familiar tightening in chest and lungs. She draws in a ragged, tearing breath, feels the building pressure at her temples, her eyes beginning to throb, her body craving air.

The others resume their song. Heightened now, purposeful, edged with bloodlust, loaded with desire.

As the girl begins to spasm and kick, she makes a strangled rasping sound. A stream of urine trickles down her legs, making rivers in the red clay, a gross inversion of menstrual blood. Her eyes are white and wild, her body bucking against the wooden frame, showering petals.

Behind the uprooted ash, her own vision blurs, prickling with bright, glittering points of light. The wind grows louder, roaring in her ears, a tornado. She feels the warm, wet seep between her own legs. *Can't breathe–Can't breathe–Can't breathe.*

The horned man is strong and certain, and it doesn't take long. As the girl loses the battle, her limbs go limp; soon she is still.

He steps back, allowing the girl's head to fall forward once more. Her body slumps against her ties like a puppet, a waxwork – some exhibit from a museum of murder. He circles his kill, raises his arms and makes an unearthly cry. His words are guttural and strange, but their tone cannot be mistaken – a solicitation, an entreaty. The others join in a cacophony of heretic calls.

As the voices swell, she is released from her own invisible binds. She comes back to herself, collapses against the dry dead roots of the ash, sucks in great lungfuls of air, presses her face against the beetle-burrowed wood, the gritty, worm-churned earth. She's shaking, heartbeat roaring, the sound of her blood melding with the wind.

Back in the clearing, people are gathering around the dead girl, taking turns to touch her, to kiss her forehead, each one glowing with a wild, reverent awe. They are rewarded for their sacrifice. But they seem unreal now, their outlines blurring, little tendrils of light seeming to spiral from each figure and float up into the treetops.

She knows she has seen what she was meant to see. It is over.

Gathering her strength, she stumbles away from her hiding place, back the way she had come, no longer noticing the brambles or nettle stings, the firelight fading behind her. She has dropped her torch, but needs no guide, each blind footstep like stepping onto a virgin planet. Her heartbeat slows. Her chest aches. Tears make glittering starlight. The trees she passes begin to fade, her fingertips no longer finding a grip on their trunks and branches. By the time she reaches her campsite, they are gone, and her tent squats there, glowing dimly in the early brightening.

Turbine 34 turns slowly, a looming dark presence. She looks out over the moor, the twinkling streetlights of the villages on distant slopes, and far off, the orange haze of a city. Her vision seems sharper, dawn colours richer, her body sings with strange vitality. She understands now – she knows, the way an animal knows. She feels no pain, no tiredness, no hunger. She is no longer afraid.

A symphony of first birdsong sounds from the valley. Nearby, the lonely call of a curlew – the orchestra's soloist. So, the curlews are still here, after all.

She thinks of the bone she found, now resting next to her sleeping bag, and the pieces of her puzzle slot into place.

Day 5

The rain starts an hour after sunrise.

Outside the red womb of the tent, the world has righted itself. She can hear Turbine 34, the whine and screech of gears, the propeller swoop of blades. The first pit pat of raindrops. She worms to the door. The morning sky is hectic with fast-moving grey clouds, pools of sunlight undulating across far hills. To the east the horizon is invisible, hidden by the dense murk of heavy rain. She sees only beauty.

Should she leave? No way. Not now. Not when she's so close.

The bone lies beside her. She hasn't bagged and tagged it, as she should have done, as she would have done before. She picks it up and runs her fingertips lovingly over its mottled surface. At one end there are hard little knots of tendon and ligament, preserved by the peat.

She climbs out of the sleeping bag, pulls on waterproofs. She needs to beat the storm.

Turbine 34 rotates slowly, the blade's tips slicing through cloud. It looks filthy in this light, she notices, without the gilding sun. A grey accumulation of pollution and weather, black stains around the rivets, oily smears of grease. Dents in the tower where protestors have used mallets. It already looks old, decrepit, another industrial relic. How long before it's abandoned, just like all the other remnants of the past – the farms, mills and grouse butts, the field walls, ditches and culverts – all the ways humans have tried and failed to shape this land and make it productive, not understanding that its purpose is simply to exist.

She watches the valley and the clouds clinging to the trees like tufts of wool caught on barbed wire. The birds have fallen silent, all except a clattering of wet-feathered jackdaws wheeling on the wind. On a distant hillside, a few miserable sheep confer in the shelter of an old dry-stone fold. Nature is hunkering down.

She hadn't covered the pit where she'd found the bone and already water is gathering in its recesses. She surveys the surrounding landscape. There's a distinct hump in the ground close by. It could be a spoil heap,

left over from the wind farm's construction, the remnants of old turbary workings, or something else. She
measures by eye and decides it's far enough beyond the
concrete foundations of Turbine 34 to discount the
former. She sinks a peat probe, and it comes up sticky
at least a metre deep. This is where she'll start.

She gathers tools: a collapsible peat spade, the trowel, plastic specimen bags. She collects the camera and
marker pen and then changes her mind. None of that
matters now. She needs to work fast. Out of habit she
marks out a two-metre squared area beside the ground
swell, pinning the tape with rocks collected from the
turbine platform.

Then, she starts to dig.

By midday the rain is heavy, splashing the back of her
neck in fat drops, and she's found nothing. The pit she's
dug is three inches in water, the surface peat too dried
out to absorb the sudden deluge. Instead, the excess
forms pools and spills into the fissures. She can hear the
gurgle of new watercourses forming beneath ground,
just as she predicted. She's too hot in the waterproofs,
sweating with effort, so she peels down to her shorts
and vest. The rain feels good on her skin. She hasn't
showered in five hot days and the water is like baptism.

In the clouds to the east, she spies flashes of distant lightening. The wind is rising. The sensible thing
would be to retreat. She could take the track past the old

farmhouse, make her way back to town. The thought is
fleeting – quickly dismissed. Stubbornness and purpose
drive her on.

She abandons the first pit and begins a fresh one
the other side of the small hillock. It's tough digging
here, complicated by decades of heather cover, the roots
woody and thick. But she persists, working into the afternoon, carefully exposing the plants, sorting through
their root systems, looking for signs.

About three feet down, she's rewarded.

She almost misses it, embedded in the peat face, small
and easily mistaken for a stone chip. Her heart tweaks as
she picks it up and turns it in her fingers. Bone. A small
one, barely more than a centimetre long.

The rain splashes in her palm as she cradles it.

She puts it carefully in a sample bag and folds it into
her pocket, then goes back to the tent and fetches a
tarpaulin, two extendable struts she'd carried for exactly this purpose, and spare tent pegs. She rigs up a
makeshift shelter over the pit. The tarpaulin flaps and
strains in the increasing wind, so she fetches stones from
the rubble heap to secure it. She brings the lantern, too,
and sets it close to where she'd found the tiny bone.

She takes the trowel and begins to scrape gently at
the peat face, protected by her makeshift shelter. It's
not long before the roots of the heather give up another
small pale fragment. She works slowly, meticulously,

ignoring the soaking shirt plastered to her back, her mud-slathered feet, the rain waterfalling over the tarpaulin.

She follows the clues the moor has revealed, carefully uncovering another slim, fragile bone, slightly longer this time. This bone is connected to another by fibrous tissue and covered in places with a tough, leathery material. She takes a moment, suddenly breathless, a knot of emotion stuck fast in her throat. The rain is coming down hard now, rattling on the tarpaulin, creating new stream beds in the animal tracks through the heather. She can't allow herself to get distracted. She was right, but she hasn't got much longer. She needs to keep going.

Alongside the first set of fragile bones, she finds more, slightly larger and, toward one end, a knuckle of leathery skin. The next is better still, three jointed bones held together with toughened sinew. The fourth is almost perfect, covered with the distinct earthy patina of preserved skin. There is even the faint shadow of a nail bed, though the nail itself is gone. Each of these is connected by shrunken tissue, brown as old cowhide. She uses her fingers to gently uncover more, wishing she had a brush, or some other implement, until it she's sure: she has uncovered a hand, lying palm up in the peat. Upon this palm she finds a miniature map:

hills and valleys, the striations of streambeds, pathways marking out the shape of a life.

She is stunned by its detail, its undeniable perfection.

She glances toward Turbine 34, blades like splayed fingers, and then she leans forward and places her own hand gently against the one in the ground. One by one, she lays her soft fleshy fingers down, presses palm to palm. Her skin seems to tingle and pulse, as if there is life within – just as she feels when she presses her hands to a tree or a rock. Perhaps it is only her own reflected lifeforce. Her own pattering heart, sending her blood careening through her veins. Her own quick, shallow breath, speaking back to her. She floods with the sensation she'd had in the night – the revelation, the conviction – and stays there for some time, remembering, while the wind shrieks, obliterating the sound of her weeping.

By the time she understood the truth of him, it was already too late.

It was mid-afternoon when she reached the ruin. Kent's Beetle was there, windscreen blinking in the sun. The only sign of him, three cigarette butts by the driver's door. Filtered, not rollies. That was unusual. Inside the ruin, she disturbed a cat who'd made a den out of their tangled blankets. The rangy body and ragged ear tips of a feral. Normally she'd try to entice it closer, but she'd no time for that today. The hard knot in her chest drove her on, up the track and onto the moor. The only place he could be.

She'd expected to see him at college – today of all days – but he hadn't shown up. She'd searched for him, checking the labs, the staff room, the car park, surrounded by the heightened cacophony of squealing, crying teenagers. Sally, hugging her and babbling about halls of residence and fresher's week.

A simple slip of paper in a brown envelope, her name in typescript, hazy through the opaque address window. Such a simple thing, so mundane, holding the keys to her future. Her fingers had trembled as she'd opened it and opened the entire world.

Then, teachers singling her out, shaking her hand. Classmates hugging her, shining with their own relief and fresh hope. The thrill of a life changed, redirected, away from the shadowed valleys and barren moors, away from stultifying boredom and bottles of Thunderbird on park benches. From tractors and sheep and the stink of manure. One girl sobbed against her mother's chest, the older woman, red-cheeked and stoic. But there was only one person she wanted to tell.

He stood near the spot they'd found the red tent that
first day. Even from a distance, he was unmistakable.
She cut from the path and made her way slowly across
the open moor, slipping in wet pockets of bog, water
seeping between her toes. She wasn't dressed for this,
still in Converse, a long cotton skirt and t-shirt. She
should've stopped back at home, but she'd been too
impatient, her task too imperative.

Their affair had continued through the spring term,
and into the hot, dry summer. Their public meetings,
loaded with secretive, meaningful glances, inevitably
ended in furtive sweaty encounters in bathrooms and
storage cupboards. But her favourite times were when
they were alone, at the old ruin, where she had gradually fashioned their own private love nest in one corner of the dilapidated kitchen. She loved their trips to
the moor, to collect soil samples, or record migrating
birdlife, when she felt most herself, able to relax and
be natural with him. During those times he too seemed
lighter, less inhibited, his unpredictable moods blasted
away by the fresh moorland wind.

But there had been little opportunity since exams
finished. Now, there was less reason to meet. Fewer
chances. She hadn't spent the holidays worrying about

A-level results, like most of her college friends, but worrying about him instead, battling the sense that he was slipping further from her grasp, and she couldn't quite get him back.

A month ago, he'd flat refused her suggestion to go public.

'But I'm not your student anymore.'

'You don't understand. People won't see it like that.'

But still, she hoped.

And now? Surely, this changed everything. She was becoming an adult. His equal.

As she neared him, her heart picked up pace. The brown envelope was folded and tucked inside a little embroidered cloth bag, slung across her chest. It might as well have been a firecracker. A match. A bomb.

He was smoking, of course, and in one hand, held the dregs of a bottle of Jack Daniel's. As she neared him, he tossed his cigarette aside and stepped on it – he knew the dangers at this time of year.

He turned to look at her, one brow cocked in a question. A whisper of irritation stopped her from stumbling into his arms.

'Well?' he asked.

'Why weren't you at college?'

He smiled, but it didn't reach his eyes. There was something cold lodged there. 'I wanted to meet you here. It seemed right. I knew you'd figure it out.'

Her heart melted at the romance, impatience floating away like a dandelion clock.

'*Well?*

She couldn't help herself. As she drew the results slip from her bag she grinned. She held it out to him, but he didn't take it.

'You did it?'

She nodded.

He placed the whisky bottle at his feet and took her by the waist. 'I knew you would.'

Tears welled in her eyes now, the unbearable tension of those last months unspooling like a dropped bobbin. 'You always said I could.'

It was true. This was all because of him.

He kissed her then, long and deep. It felt different.

He drew back and took the results slip from her, glanced at it, folded it and slipped it into his jeans pocket. He looked out toward the horizon, then took both her hands in his, sighing deeply. 'So, I guess this is it then.'

'What?'

'This is the end of the road, isn't it?' His eyes shone like wet stones as he gazed at her.

'What are you talking about?'

'Well, this changes everything.'

His words, echoing her thoughts.

'In a good way...'

He smiled again, humouring her, but it was an empty smile, as empty as the moor around them. 'My darling, surely you knew that if this happened, it would mean the end for us.'

She tugged her hands from his. She'd misheard, surely. Misunderstood. 'No. I thought ... Why are you being like this?'

'Like what?'

'All weird and sad. Are you pissed?'

'No, I'm not pissed.'

'Then why are you saying this?'

He sighed, a little exasperated, as if she were too stupid, too young, to understand.

'You didn't think this was forever, did you? You're not *that* naïve.'

'I thought—'

'Look...' he took up her hands again. 'This has been fun, but it has to end now. You must see that. I ...we just can't risk anyone finding out.'

'But I don't care who knows. I love you.' The words – never quite said until now – had sat on her tongue for months. She felt sick, body crawling with white hot shock. He didn't mean it. He couldn't.

He seemed to hesitate a moment, then stepped close again, pulled her into his arms. She pressed her face against his shoulder, kissed his neck. She had to find a way to reach him, to change his mind. She slid her hand inside the fly of his jeans, felt him harden.

'I'm sorry,' he whispered into her hair. 'I'm so sorry, but it has to be this way.'

His hands on her skin were gentle at first, then firm and insistent, his whisky breath coming faster, as if her distress had loosed something in him. Salt and smoke and sex in his kiss.

She clung to him as he pushed her down onto the heather. She needed him. Needed to know she was still his. She'd do anything. Then he was on top of her, between her legs, sharp hips bruising her thighs. He was all over her, inside her, her mind blank of anything but him. His sun-warmed back, his wet mouth, his hard, lean body, those beautiful pale hands – on her skin, in her hair, tightening at her throat.

Night

Darkness falls early. The storm comes.

The rain becomes a deluge, the sky churns. Old springs are reborn, streams and rivulets forging new paths between heather beds, tracking the ancient routes of grouse and stoat.

The pit begins to fill, disrupting her work, so she digs fresh drainage channels, directing the waterflow away. She fetches chunks of concrete and stones from the rubble pile and creates a makeshift dam on the uphill lip of the pit, a flood wall in miniature. She reinforces the tarpaulin by hefting the heaviest rocks over the tent pegs. Water seeps in anyway, trickles down the peat face, pools in the hollows, but she's done what she can. She fetches a torch and headlamp to supplement the lantern, creating a luminous sanctuary. It's cold now, but she doesn't notice, inured to the constant damp, the rebellious wind. The weather will win eventually, but she's given herself more time.

Turbine 34's blades are still. The turbines switch off automatically in high winds, for fear that the forces they are meant to harness will tear them apart, limb by limb. She stares at it. Against the turbulent sky, it is a black, sinister shadow. Grating metallic straining and rattling cuts above the wind. Screeches of distress. Or perhaps warning.

In the valley, the flood siren wails. Its air-raid lament has always sent chills spiralling through her body. It's a sound she associates with bombs, wars, nuclear annihilation, indoctrinated by Cold War fears bred into her. It will not take such human extremity for destruction to come. She ignores it and hunkers in the relative safety of her shelter.

Beneath the tarpaulin, the torso is now exposed.

The ribs are covered by a chrysalis of brown leathery skin, shrivelled breasts like pieces of jerky. In places the flesh has decomposed, exposing the umber struts of ribs. As she traces them with her fingertips, she senses the steady expansion and contraction of lungs, the soft whisper of a heartbeat.

She works on, methodologically uncovering the shoulder joints, and, as she expected, a space where a humerus bone should be. She fetches the bone she'd found and lays it gently in place, then removes the tiny finger chip from her pocket and nestles it next to its mate. She feels a deep sense of absolution. This act of reunification is the completion of a macabre puzzle, a kind of atonement that makes tears prick at her eyes.

She decides to work down the body, peeling peat away to reveal the pelvis, which has been crushed and flattened by the pressure of the bog. Small curls of hair are still attached to the skin above the pubis. The muscle-covered hips are strangely smooth, narrow curves evident. The legs are easier to uncover and identify, large femur bones intact, tendons and tissues present, the kind of legs formed by years of walking up hills, over crag and marsh, up the steep ridges of wooded valleys.

The feet have fared less well. One is missing altogether, the other misshapen, a few of the smaller bones scattered. She searches carefully, retrieving tarsals, laying them gently in an approximation of where they should be.

And still the rain falls.

It must be cold, but she can't feel it. She must be hungry, but she can't feel that either.

Above, the sky flashes, the crash and roar of thunder coming closer.

Count it: one-two-three-four. One-two.

Turbine 34, illuminated by lightning, is revealed as a grotesque with accusatory pointing fingers. It seems to loom toward her, as if it might bend and prod her with those fiberglass blades. The outline of the surrounding moor looks different too. She has come to know the lay of the land, but suddenly, contours seem unfamiliar. She could swear there's a rise in the land to the north, where before it was flat. A trick of the mind? Distorted vision? She's not sure. She no longer trusts what she sees.

It's then she hears a low rumbling. She pauses in her work, listens. It comes again – a deep, fractious growl, coming from the earth beneath. She presses an ear to the peat. A vibration ripples through her body. Something is stirring, deep below. A tight knot in her chest tells her to hurry. She doesn't have much time.

She works quickly now, uncovering the skull. The jawbone is still intact, with the narrow profile of a female. The teeth are good, surprisingly straight and sound. There's a cavity where a nose should be; over the eyes, thin flaps of eyelid. Sunken, gaunt cheeks, shrivelled death-mask lips. Most of the cranium is exposed, but clumps of dark hair lay matted like rotten rushes.

When she has cleared enough, she sits back on her haunches. She is covered in filth, limbs slippery with mud and rain, hair dripping, thick smears across her cheeks.

The girl – for that is how she thinks of her – the girl looks so peaceful. There's no hint of struggle. It's as if she had simply lain herself down and allowed the bog to consume her. Except perhaps, if she looks closely, the faint suggestion of markings about the neck.

A great swell of regret and compassion forces tears. She's sorry that she could not stop what happened to her.

A loud, raging groan sounds from somewhere deep in the earth. She feels a tremor, an unnerving vibration beneath her knees. She peers out across the moor to Turbine 34. It looks all wrong. The blades sit at an odd angle, the tower on a slant, the nacelle's nose tilted toward the ground like a downed aircraft.

She sends the torch beam toward it but is blinded by rain like silver splinters. She flicks it off, waits for lightning. When it comes, she sees what she feared. To the north of Turbine 34, the land has begun to shift and rise, as the huge concrete foundation is undermined. Again, a deafening groan, as if the earth is writhing in pain. She sees the moment the moor begins to move, subtle at first, a slow shifting, almost undetectable and disconcerting, like looking through the wrong lens. She knows what this is, and she knows what will happen.

The bog will burst and spill down the hillside, destroying everything in its path. It will fell trees and poison rivers and take livestock and homes and bodies with it. It is indiscriminate, caring nothing for human life or human endeavour. Nature has no mercy. It will yawn and stretch and resettle itself, like an old barn tom, concerned by nothing but its own primal desires.

She stares at the girl in the ground, a fierce and sudden need rising – she could not protect her then, but she can protect her now.

She tosses the torch aside, peels off her drenched shorts, underwear and vest, unhooks her worn-out sports bra, and lays down. Carefully, she places herself breast to breast, hip to hip, feels the hard press of bone, the slipperiness of wet leathered skin, the intimate contours of a human body. A heartbeat not her own. It's been so long, but the familiarity is instantly soothing. Tension drains from her limbs, bleeds into the peat. The peat that will spit out its secrets.

She breathes.

In: one-two

Out: one-two-three-four.

I am safe. I am safe. I am safe.

It feels so right. She doesn't know why she fought it for so long.

The earth makes a deafening, thunderous roar as the bog bursts and begins to slide. The moor quakes as Turbine 34 falls, uprooted like a downed tree.

Softly, she places a single kiss on the girl's bony, beautiful skull, then lays her head down, cheek to cheek. Her heartbeat slows, matching the rhythm against her chest. Her breath ebbs, mirroring the subtle rise and fall. Skeletal arms wrap around her, drawing her close. Toughened palms press to her spine. The girl smells elemental. Of peat fires and starlit nights, of deer meat roasting over flame, of rabbit skins and sphagnum moss, of fresh cut oak and damp red clay, of sheep fleece and afterbirth, of curlew nests and fox shit, of summer dust and crowberries, of cotton grass and heather pollen, of rotting leaf-fall and pheasant feathers, of gunpowder and gun smoke, of diesel fuel and wet dog, of the cold northerly wind and the metallic taint of snow and the diamond glitter of waterfalls, of cigarettes and male sweat and whisky breath.

She can rest now. She is home.

Acknowledgements

This book was inspired by the campaign to prevent the construction of an industrial-scale wind farm on the protected peatlands of Walshaw Moor, West Yorkshire. At the time of writing, controversial proposals remain in place to turn this rare landscape into England's largest onshore wind farm. These blanket peat bogs store carbon, provide crucial habitats for endangered wildlife, help protect local communities from flooding, and are part of a rich cultural and literary heritage, not least as the much-loved Brontë country.

I acknowledge the influence of the dedicated work of campaigners, in particular Mark Avery for his informative blog, and Christopher Godden, whose guest post inspired the title of this book.

However, Turbine 34 is a work of fiction. All characters and locations are imagined. Any errors or inaccuracies are entirely mine.

Huge thanks to Ariell Cacciola for the opportunity, for her sharp editorial insight, and for championing the work of Northern writers. Sincere thanks also to Luisa Dias for the striking jacket design, and to Paddy Wells and Jan Clements for invaluable early feedback and encouragement.

And finally, heartfelt thanks to my writing community – especially members of The Inkwell, whose generosity supports my writing, and all those who joined me for 100 Days of Writing in 2024. I wrote this book alongside you.

About the Author

Katherine Clements is the author of three historical novels: *The Crimson Ribbon*, *The Silvered Heart* and *The Coffin Path* which became an Amazon bestseller and was nominated for the HWA Gold Crown Award and The Guardian's Not the Booker Prize in 2018.

She is a Royal Literary Fund Fellow, having held fellowships at both Sheffield and Manchester Universities, and a Fulbright Scholar. She is currently completing her forth novel which was birthed during a Fulbright funded year living in New Orleans. Katherine was editor of Historia, the online magazine of the Historical Writers' Association and, for three years was commissioning editor at the Royal Literary Fund magazine Collected where she worked with many prize-winning and bestselling writers.

She is based in West Yorkshire where she runs her own business as a writing coach and mentor.

Instagram @katherineclementswriter
Substack www.katherineclements.substack.com
Website www.katherineclements.co.uk

About The Northern Weird Project

This book is a part of The Northern Weird Project by Wild Hunt Books, a collection of six pocket-sized novellas by authors who are writing and living in the North of England.

Incorporating eerie and uncanny incidents, these novellas investigate aspects of the North through setting, subject and character.

All books in this series are available to order from our bookshop.
https://www.wildhuntbooks.co.uk/bookshop

More From The Northern Weird Project

This House Isn't Haunted But We Are
by Stephen Howard

Simon and Priya's young daughter has died in a tragic accident. Determined to heal their fracturing marriage, the couple move to the North Yorkshire Moors to renovate a dilapidated rural cottage. However, they just can't process their grief as increasingly eerie events unfold. A child's ghostly figure appears on the moors, doors lock themselves, and a mysterious stain grows from the loft. Is it their daughter haunting them or something else?

(Don't) Call Mum
by Matt Wesolowski

Leo is just trying to catch his train back home to the village of Malacstone in North East England. But there's disorder at the station, and when a loud young man heading for London boards the train accidentally, a usually easy journey descends into darkness and chaos. The train soon breaks down in the middle of nowhere, and as night falls, something...or someone steps out of the distance. Is it a man or something far more sinister?

The Off-Season
by Jodie Robins

It's the off-season in the seaside resort town of Blackpool, where Tommy never imagined he would return. His relationship has broken down, so he returns home to keep an eye on his widowed father. While counting down the hours before attending the funeral of a well-loved friend, a mysterious group turns up on the seafront. One by one, the locals are entranced by their presence until Tommy and his father can no longer resist the allure. Tommy soon discovers a secret desire his father has been harbouring for his entire life.

The Retreat
by Gemma Fairclough

Richard's sister Julie returns home from a mysterious wellness facility in remote Cumbria in 1994. He's convinced that this place was a cult and was the cause of his sister's eventual suicide. Finally, after years as an unaccomplished academic, he decides to investigate the disturbing accusations against the Hartman Retreat Centre. Then he meets Lucy, a young woman whose story is eerily similar to his sister's decades before. Richard is determined to unearth what's really been happening at the Hartman Retreat Centre but more importantly, who is Charles Hartman, the celebrated healer who casts a powerful hold over all who come to the retreat.

Good Boy
by Neil McRobert

After a boy vanishes on the outskirts of a small Northern town, a woman spies from her window a mysterious man digging a grave in the exact spot of the disappearance. However, when she confronts him, the man's true purpose is far more chilling than she could have imagined and the history of the town's fatal past unfolds. What has been hiding in this small northern town all these years? A gripping story of supernatural horror, nostalgia and mystery.

Wild Hunt Books would like to thank the following
Lifetime Supporters:

Daniel Sorabji
Jan Penovich
Blaise Cacciola

BECOME A SUPPORTER BY CONTACTING US AT
INFO@WILDHUNTBOOKS.CO.UK

The Publisher would also like to thank the following
early supporters of The Northern Weird Project:

Aidan Smith
Alex Herod
Ali W
Alicia Lomas-Gross
Anthony Martin
Beth Baskett
Bethany Vare
Blair Rose
Carmen
Charlotte Platt
Charlotte Tierney
Emma Armshaw
Freya S
George Dunn
Heidi Marjamäki
Ianthe May
J. Aaron Courts CWO4, USMC, Retired
Jeff
Jennifer B. Lyday
K. Wicks
Kelsey Stoddard
Kirsty Logan
Laura Elliott
Lisa Elliott

Lynne G

Mandy Bublitz

Mark Taylor

Martyn Waites

Monica Voynovska

Nicola Leedham

Nina Woodcock

Rachel Bridgeman

Rosie Warfield

Samuel Best

Sheena E. Perez

Sonja Zimmermann

Sophy Holland

Stefanie Olivola

Stephanie Eleanor Henrichs Welch

Stewart Mack

Vince Fairclough